Tofu
and
T. rex

Tofu
and
T. rex

GREG LEITICH SMITH

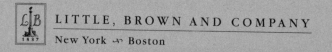

LITTLE, BROWN AND COMPANY
New York ‹› Boston

Also by Greg Leitich Smith:
Ninjas, Piranhas, and Galileo

Little, Brown and Company

Time Warner Book Group
1271 Avenue of the Americas, New York, NY 10020
Visit our Web site at www.lb-kids.com

First Edition: July 2005

Library of Congress Cataloging-in-Publication Data

Smith, Greg Leitich.
Tofu and T. rex / by Greg Leitich Smith. — 1st ed.
    p.   cm.
Summary: Hans-Peter, who enjoys working in his family's Chicago deli-
catessen, applies for admission to the prestigious Peshtigo School, where
his cousin Freddie, a vegan and outspoken animal rights activist, attends.
ISBN 0-316-77722-6
[1. Cousins — Fiction. 2. Schools — Fiction. 3. Delicatessens — Fiction.
4. Veganism — Fiction. 5. Vegetarianism — Fiction. 6. Chicago (Ill.) —
Fiction.] I. Title.
PZ7.S6488To 2005
[Fic] — dc22

                                        2004023515

Cover photo by Michael Wang

10 9 8 7 6 5 4 3 2 1
                Q-FF
Printed in the United States of America

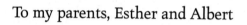
To my parents, Esther and Albert

Tofu
and
T. rex

Chapter 1

Eat Your Vegetables

Freddie

It wasn't *my* fault they had to re-sod the football field.

Mostly.

Eric Sanchez — the only other vegan in my school — and I had only taken action because the school district hadn't listened to our entirely reasonable objections to trotting out this poor, ancient, drugged-up steer as live mascot for adherents of the rabid and inhumane cult of football. Angus, the so-called "Fighting Angus," could barely stand in the mid-August heat of our first-day-of-classes "pep rally." We figured he'd probably keel over altogether on opening day.

The plan was for Eric and me to sneak out to the high school football stadium, and use some paint thinner and matches to burn SAVE ME! onto the turf. The grass would turn brown just in time for kickoff, and it would look like Angus was crying out for help, mercy, respect, and salvation. The turf would grow back, no permanent harm done, and our message would be delivered to all the Friday night spectators. It might even have made the local TV news.

We didn't plan on getting caught.

The school district was going to press charges for desecrating hallowed ground, but my parents offered to replace the whole thing with brand-new grass, install a sprinkler system (free of charge), and make a donation to the school library.

Being strapped for cash after just having spent a couple million bucks on the stadium's new Jumbo-tron, the school district accepted.

I, however, had been expelled and my parents had been told that, after my blasphemy, it would be safer for me to leave the Republic of Texas. That's why I was on a flight to Chicago, to restart eighth grade back at the Peshtigo School and live with my grandfather and cousin's family.

❋

Hans-Peter

"Do it that way and you will lose a finger," Opa told me while I was wiping residue from Westphalian ham off the slicing machine. He held the grounded three-prong electrical plug in front of me. "Always, you must unplug it first."

Since I'd been hearing my grandfather's digits-in-the-cold-cuts horror stories for as long as I could remember, I just grunted and kept cleaning. Opa insisted that the machinery and the food prep surfaces be kept extraordinarily sanitary, under his close supervision, of course. I worked most afternoons at Delicatessen Kowalski with him and a couple of longtime family friends/employees who, like me, had heard all his stories about kitchen hazards and accidental maimings. Fortunately, this once, before Opa could get too far into the disturbing tale of his second cousin Reinhard, the cleaver, and the *kasseler rippchen,* the phone rang. A couple seconds later, the fax machine signaled incoming.

"Finish," Opa said, then went up front to answer the bells.

By the time the slicer was clean enough not only to pass health inspection, but Opa's as well, he came back around the meat counter and announced, "You will be having a sister."

Because you could never tell with my grandfather's sense of humor, I asked the first thing that came to mind. "Who's the father?"

In response, he whacked me on the head with his Cubs cap. "Watch what you say about your mother," he warned.

My mother is America's only licensed, freelance *fugu* chef. Fugu is, of course, Japanese, and is not available in these United States. It is a type of sushi made from the blowfish, whose liver contains a poison several times more toxic than arsenic. Unless properly prepared, it will kill you. Rapidly, but painfully.

Mom is something of a celebrity in Japan, possibly because she's American of Polish-German descent and was once married to a (Japanese) minor league baseball player. Periodically, Mom spends several weeks in Tokyo charging exorbitant fees to affluent, thrill-seeking baseball fans who like raw fish and have a death wish. She had, in fact, left on just such a trip a few weeks ago and wasn't scheduled to be back until late October.

So, anyway, I still thought Opa was joking about the whole "sister" thing because fugu chefing was probably one of those things, like asbestos removal or ingesting large quantities of Bavarian alcoholic beverages, that shouldn't be done while pregnant. Also, my parents have been divorced ten years, and Mom never dates.

"I didn't say anything about Mom," I told Opa, playing along, "and shouldn't *she* be the one telling me this?" I wiped my hands on a paper towel, then crumpled it up and tossed it into the garbage.

Opa sighed. "You're not having a *real* sister," he said. "Your cousin Frederika will be staying with us." He peered at the slicer, then made the grunting noise he makes when he finds it sufficiently antiseptic. "She will be going back to Peshtigo School this fall."

This was bad news. Really, appallingly bad. My cousin Freddie — full name Frederika Viktoria Murchison-Kowalski — and her parents had moved down to a ranch outside Austin, Texas, last year just after Christmas, where they had planned to raise hay and donkeys. My grandfather thought this was less than a good idea, largely because the only thing my Uncle Theobald, Opa's son (a retired commodities broker), knew about donkeys was that they were mammals. As for Aunt Mary, she was a nice lady and a certified Master Gardener.

Freddie, their only child, was just certifiable. She always wore black, including lipstick, and was always doing these deeply disturbing things that would have gotten anyone normal — like me — into heaps of trouble or sent away to military academy in someplace like Manitoba.

"Wait a second," I said as the news registered. "*This* fall? You mean Freddie is going to be here in . . . in three days?" It was four days until school began here.

Opa put his hat back on. "*Nein,*" he said. "That was your aunt. Frederika is on the airplane. She will be here in three hours."

I mentally connected the dots. Fast. "She's *not* getting the back bedroom," I said. We lived in your typical early-twentieth century Chicago three-bedroom, brick bungalow, although the attic had been finished out into Opa's apartment. Mom and I each had a bedroom. The third one, behind the kitchen, was a home office, where Mom and I shared the computer and printer. Mostly, though, it was filled with my bestiary of prehistoric animals and *T. rex* collectibles.

"Frederika will have the back bedroom," Opa replied firmly. "We will move your dinosaurs and computer machines to the basement."

"We could put Freddie in the basement," I suggested.

"The basement is not habitable," Opa replied.

I was not happy, but with my bookcases already filled with books and frog tanks, there really wasn't any extra space in my room, and there was no way Mom would let me set up in the dining room. The basement did have space, technically, but it was unfinished, usually damp year-round, unheated and chilly in the winter, and largely occupied by the life-sized papier-mache *Tyrannosaurus rex* head Opa and I had built a couple years ago to see if *T. rex* really had been big enough to swallow a person whole.

It was.

As we locked up and headed out to Opa's VW, he spelled it out for me. "So you and Frederika will both be freshmen at Peshtigo School next year."

Opa was being optimistic. The Peshtigo School was this private school down by Lake Shore Drive and the Ogden Slip. It had been around since just after the Great Chicago Fire. The school had a reputation for being very good at just about everything, and was also nationally recognized for being quirky, bizarre, and nontraditional.

"Progressive," the Web site said.

Freddie, of course, had been going there since kindergarten. Me, I'd just sent in my preliminary application for admissions for high school at Peshtigo because, well, I wanted to be able to get away with half the things Freddie does.

Not really.

Actually, it's because they have this terrific paleontology program. Yeah, it's kind of odd for a high school to offer paleontology, even as an elective, but that's the Peshtigo School. They have this fantastic project where you get to spend the summer in Montana exploring the fossil beds. There are even rumors they're trying to set up a similar program in Mongolia (if they can get the State Department to agree), where paleontologists are making some great therizinosaurus finds.

So I was applying.

The Peshtigo School admissions process, though, was legendary, difficult, and mysterious. Mysterious, as in it was almost impossible to find out anything about it. I actually knew one or two people who attended the Peshtigo School, but they'd clammed up as soon as they found out I was applying. Like it was some kind of strange, sinister, secret conspiracy.

But of course Freddie had gotten in and must have been re-admitted.

And there was an excellent chance I could grill her for some information.

I leaned back into the bucket seat. "Are you sure we can't put Freddie in the basement?" I asked. It was the perfect environment in which to conduct an interrogation.

"You will be nice to your cousin," Opa ordered, then put the car in gear.

Freddie

Because the people at O'Hare Airport apparently can't make the planes run on time, my flight was late getting in and took another eternity to make it to the gate.

This meant I had an additional seventy-eight minutes to listen to the guy next to me talk on the air phone. He was on his way to a homebuilders convention at McCormick Place and extremely concerned with the relative merits of various brands of reciprocating saws when used for the demolition phase of an old home remodel.

Being stuck there, listening to him, almost made me understand how some animals can gnaw off their own limbs when caught in a steel-jawed trap.

When I finally escaped from the plane, I made my way down to baggage claim.

I spotted them before they spotted me: a short, gray-haired eastern European man in a Cubs cap and a medium-sized, somewhat nerdy-looking kid without one. Opa and my cousin Hans-Peter were waiting in front of the luggage dispenser.

And I was going to be living with them.

The whole situation was very last-minute, and it would take getting used to. My parents, though, had made it clear that Opa was in charge and, being from the old country, was less tolerant of "shenanigans" than they were. They'd also told me not to antagonize Hans-Peter too much, since he'd never had a sibling before.

Of course, I hadn't either.

"Senator!" Opa bellowed. (I had asked him some time ago not to call me "Princess," because it made me sound like a poodle or someone who wore a lot of pink. Also, I don't believe in hereditary monarchy.) "Senator!" Opa bellowed again.

This caused one or two people to stare.

I ignored them.

After I hugged Opa and greeted Hans-Peter, Opa asked, "Did the airline give you good food? Have you eaten?"

"No," I said, "and no." I'd declined the honey-roasted cashews because of the bees, but even if I hadn't been vegan, the chicken alfredo had looked like it had been stored in formaldehyde a bit too long.

"We will go to Do Your Wurst," Opa declared.

It was his favorite restaurant, a major customer of the family deli, owned by friends, and conveniently located two doors down from Delicatessen Kowalski.

"I'm a vegan now," I said, because last year I was only an ovo-lacto vegetarian and because I thought they should know immediately and because Do Your Wurst was probably the least vegan-friendly restaurant in the entire city.

After a pause, Opa asked, "Is that healthy?"

"Extremely," I told him, even though that really wasn't the point. "No animal products. No meat. No eggs. No dairy. Nothing that results from the exploitation of fellow sentient beings. It's good for them. It's *very* good for you."

Hans-Peter made a face.

Opa shook his head. "I have read about this," he said. "Soy milk. Beans. Birdseed." He waved a hand dismissively. "Ach! It will never catch on."

"No, really," I told him, although I didn't honestly expect to make any headway. At least not right away. "Do you know just how abused and tortured and cruelly exploited animals are? And for no good reason! It takes three *thousand* head of formerly alive cattle to provide game balls for one season of major league football."

"NFL," Hans-Peter corrected. "That's 'National Football League.' Unless you're talking about college football, in which case it's —"

"I don't care," I interrupted, because what the tyrants called themselves really wasn't what was important. "And chickens!" I went on. "The conditions at egg factories are so awful the hens are driven to *peck* each other to death!"

Opa was unusually quiet for a moment.

"Ja, well," he said, finally, as we grabbed my luggage. "Your parents have told me about this Austin." He cleared his throat, then went on. "I think you have been living in that hippie place with the bean sprouts too long. Tonight, we will go to Do Your Wurst and you will remember what real food is."

Hans-Peter

In the car going out to O'Hare, and then waiting for Freddie in baggage claim, I'd had time to get used to the idea of having her live with us. I'd even convinced myself it wouldn't be so terrible. True, she'd always been a bit extreme, but when she was around, family functions were certainly never dull. And my chances of getting in to Peshtigo might have just gone up.

Getting her to help, though, or just talking politely, would require a certain finesse.

"So," I said to Freddie from the front seat of the Beetle, "what's with this vegan thing?" Before she'd gone down to Texas, she'd been a vegetarian, which had been bad enough. This, though, could only be worse. Both at home and at the deli.

Opa was taking it remarkably calmly. Of course, that was his usual reaction to Freddie's adventures.

"Was it cholesterol, perhaps?" Opa interjected, glancing up to look at Freddie through the rearview mirror. "That is something your generation is concerned about, yes?"

"Veganism is not about lowering cholesterol," Freddie said, "although that can be a benefit. Veganism is about treating animals with respect, allowing them to live in peace and freedom. We do not eat animals. We do not steal from animals. We do not make things like clothing or lamps out of animals."

"Then it is a good thing," Opa said after a moment of silence, "that the seat you are in was made of only the finest vinyl-ocerous hide."

As usual, neither Freddie nor I laughed at Opa's joke, despite his chuckling.

"Okay," I said. "I get that you eat only vegetables, but what about mice and bugs and rats and stuff?"

"I do not like mice and bugs and rats," Freddie said, "although I respect them."

I knew Freddie didn't like small rodents because of a traumatic childhood incident, but that didn't really answer my question.

"Yes, well," I followed up, "but aren't some of them going to die from pesticides and from when you harvest the soybeans and vegetables?"

"First of all," Freddie said, "vegans do not use pesticides. We eat only organic foods. Second, we try to avoid needless suffering, while recognizing that some death is inevitable when you engage in agriculture. Things happen. We aren't perfect."

"Oh," I said, but I was a little confused. "Wait. Why is a death during harvesting not worse than just taking honey from bees or eggs from a chicken?"

She didn't hesitate. "Because there's a firm, moral difference between exploiting something to death and doing your best to avoid causing harm to other living beings."

Opa snorted. I must not have looked convinced, either, because Freddie went on. "Look, you wouldn't bash in your neighbor's head and eat out his brains just because you felt like it, would you?"

I hesitated, but not because I liked Mr. Periwinkle.

"Would you?" Freddie pressed.

I hesitated again. "Well, I mean, if we were . . . lost in a lifeboat thousands of miles from land, drifting in the wrong direction, and starving, and it was the only food available . . . I might," I replied. "But I probably wouldn't eat his brains. You know, because of that cannibal laughing sickness."

Freddie made the noise of the deeply appalled, although she didn't like Mr. Periwinkle either. "You are totally missing my point," Freddie said. "And remind me never to travel with you." She made one or two more noises of revulsion, then went on. "The point is, ordinarily, it's not something you'd do. And it's something you'd have to think long and carefully about. Even if you were in a lifeboat and he was already dead."

Okay, sure. "Yeah."

"Then extend the way you treat your fellow human beings to how you should treat *everything*," Freddie replied. "That's the vegan way."

Then she turned her whole body so that she was facing the window.

Conversation over.

Welcome back to Chicago.

The rest of the way to the restaurant, Opa filled most of the silence, talking about plans for expanding the prepared-foods section of the deli, the weather, weekend drivers, and asking Freddie what her parents were up to.

Do Your Wurst hadn't changed since sometime around 1960, or maybe earlier. The walls had dark wood paneling, covered with German beer signs and banners and autographed black-and-white photos of people like

Frank Sinatra, Richard J. Daley, and Mike Royko. There was also a bar at the back and doors that led out to the summer beer garden.

When we walked in, all the regulars fussed over Freddie, which she actually allowed. Freddie even acted almost like a normal person until she got the menu. "*Leberkäse*. . . . meatballs . . . smoked pork loin . . . veal . . . marinated beef . . . boiled pork shank . . . bratwurst," she translated. "Opa, there is absolutely nothing here I can eat!"

He stared at her over his reading glasses. "You have always eaten here!" he replied. "You can have what you always have . . . stuffed cabbage . . . there is no meat there . . . it always was your favorite."

"With mashed potatoes made from *milk*!" Freddie replied. "And I wasn't a vegan then!"

"Freddie's a vegan now," I told Gisela, who was waiting on our table, in case she hadn't heard.

"So," Opa said, glancing over a menu he knew by heart, "perhaps then you will not be having the steak tartare, but what about the creamed herring?"

"Dead fish," Freddie replied in her stubborn voice. "In a sauce made from stuff stolen from a cow."

Opa let out a deep, east European sigh. "Very well, what about this?" he said, then turned to Gisela. "Frederika would like the boiled potato and red cabbage, no butter, and a garden salad. No dressing. Is that not good?"

Gisela dutifully wrote down the order, but only after making eye contact with Freddie to confirm.

"Hans-Peter will have —"

"Sauerbraten," I interjected. Opa did tend to go a bit over the top when ordering. "And also a garden salad."

Freddie rolled her eyes.

"Hey," I told her. "Roughage is good."

"And I . . . ," Opa continued, ignoring me. "Does the five meat Bavarian dinner still come with the pork knuckles?"

"Willi," Gisela said, with a grin, "it comes with whatever you want." Freddie cringed.

"Then I will have that," Opa said. "Also, the chicken liver appetizer. Oh, and the special lager."

"Anything else?" Gisela asked, pen poised.

Opa gestured. "I almost forgot," he said. "What is the soup of the day?"

"You'll love it," Gisela replied. *"Czernina,"* she said, lingering over the word. "It's especially good today."

Freddie made a choking sound. I didn't, but duck's blood soup is not one of my favorites. A Polish delicacy, it's what my mother calls an "acquired taste."

Opa pursed his lips. "Does Hannes make it today?"

Gisela nodded. "Of course. You know we don't let Rudi near it anymore."

"Very good," Opa said, thumping the table for emphasis. "I will have it."

Gisela took the order, then headed back to the kitchen.

This left Freddie, Opa, and me staring at one another across the table.

"So," Opa said, finally, and opened the file folder he'd been carrying since we'd gotten out of the car. He looked at me over his half glasses. "This does not concern you." It was what he said at home when he and Mom were about to discuss something deeply interesting. It meant I was supposed to go to my room and pretend I couldn't hear.

"Okay," I said, then stayed put, because I wasn't going to hang out in the men's room or at the bar.

Freddie scowled, then said with conviction, "I have nothing to hide."

"Of course," Opa replied, then told Freddie. "Your mother sent me a fax with your school papers — transcripts — and why you were expelled . . . one week into the semester . . ."

Freddie held her chin high. "And?"

"And also the Peshtigo School schedule," Opa continued. He peered at Freddie until it was plain she wasn't going to say anything. Then he cleared his throat. "It appears that you have too much free time."

Freddie's eyes narrowed, but she didn't argue.

"So," Opa went on, "after school, you will work at the delicatessen with Hans-Peter and me, unless you have other activities, like —"

"I have other activities," Freddie said, quickly. "Lots. I founded the Peshtigo School chapter of the Union of Students Concerned About Cruelty to Animals and —"

"*Ausgezeichnet!*" Opa said with a broad smile, tapping the papers in front of him with an index finger. "So, when you are not working at the delicatessen, you and your club could be building a float for this . . . what do they call it?" He peered at the fax. "Homecoming parade."

"Which is a pagan ritual involving worship of the football team and alumni donations," Freddie said reflexively, then pinched her lips together in a thin black line.

"I understand," Opa said, nodding his head. "Maybe, then, you will be entering the Wurst Is Best contest during Wurstfest this year, like Hans-Peter always does."

"Sausage making?" Freddie asked. "I don't think so —"

"No?" Opa said. There was a pause. "You are certain?"

Freddie closed her eyes. "I'll do a float for the parade."

"*Wunderbar!*" Opa said as Gisela arrived with the drinks.

Chapter 2

Eat Your Meat

Freddie

When we arrived, I guess, *home* now, Opa and Hans-Peter helped bring in my luggage. A garment bag, a suitcase, and a carry-on. The rest of my stuff was being shipped.

My new bedroom was back behind the kitchen, across from the door to the basement, which had a little pet door in it for Opa's cat. I do not approve of pets. On the other hand, I approve less of mice.

The room itself was, at least, vegan-friendly. The rug was made from three kinds of synthetic and plant fibers; the sheets were made from cotton; the pillow was made from foam; and the drapes were linen.

The house itself was very North Side Chicago, very Bungalow Belt, and just a few houses down from the river. The usual size, on a typical narrow lot, with a separate garage facing the back alley. The living room was up front, with the dining room and kitchen on one side. Hans-Peter's room was next to the kitchen, separated by the stairs to the attic, which led up to Opa's apartment. The only downstairs bathroom was between the master and Hans-Peter's bedroom, with a door opening to the hall.

After unpacking and taking in my new accommodations in the home of *Wurstmeister* Kowalski, and making a note to call my friend Eleanor Mancini about the homecoming float, I threw myself into bed.

I was exhausted but too wired to fall asleep right away. I was also a little frustrated but not completely surprised by how my arrival had gone. Hans-Peter acted just like everyone else about veganism, not understanding it wasn't just some fad associated with dingbat celebrities. As for Opa, he usually let me do my own thing, but it would be hard to be true to the principles of veganism living here. Bratwurst was his life.

Hans-Peter

Next morning, Opa was at his usual spot at the kitchen table, doing his *Trib* crossword puzzle, while I was at the stove frying the bacon. Opa was a morning person. I wasn't, but it had been my chore to make weekend breakfasts for the past couple years, ever since my Mom had told me that since she was a licensed chef and Opa was

Polish-German, if I ever wanted anything as mundane as waffles, scrambled eggs, or bacon ever again, I would have to make it myself.

Freddie emerged from the back bedroom. "Bacon, huh?" she said, bleary-eyed and yawning.

"Not only bacon," Opa replied, looking around his newspaper, "the leanest cuts from rare Pomeranian wild boar. Also, very fresh."

"Isn't a Pomeranian a kind of dog?" Freddie asked.

Opa grimaced. "That, yes, but also the region on the Baltic Sea between the Oder and Vistula Rivers. Perhaps you have heard of them?"

"No," Freddie said, but I could tell she wasn't really interested in northeastern European geography. She yawned again. "By the way," she said, generally, "what was that extremely loud noise last night?"

"The El?" Opa suggested.

The El crossed the river half a block down, and the trains made a lot of noise.

"No," Freddie replied. "This was more . . . animal-sounding."

"Oh, that would be Euclid and Pythagoras," I said. "They croak."

She blinked. "That would make them what, ancient Greek frogs?"

"Bullfrogs," I told her. I didn't tell her they were just there for the summer and would be going back to my old math classroom as soon as school started. "Sometimes they get a little loud. You get used to it."

"They eat meat, *and* they keep pets," she muttered, then headed to the bathroom. A couple minutes later, she emerged, looking more ready to face us carnivores. At least she was wearing her black makeup.

"You cook animals," she said to me, staring hard at the sizzling bacon.

"I eat," I replied. "Therefore, I cook. Animals."

"He's a quick learner, too," Opa interjected. "It only took him a year to figure out how not to burn water." Opa chuckled at his own joke, while Freddie and I stayed silent. "Children today," Opa said, shaking his head and returning to his newspaper. "They have no sense of humor."

I grabbed the pair of tongs to lift the bacon strips out of the frying pan. Then I waved them at Freddie, grease dripping, before setting them onto some paper towels. "Bacon . . . yum . . ."

"The nitrates are going to kill you," she said. "Soon."

I didn't reply. Instead, I poured out some grease from the pan into a cup, set the pan back on the burner, then poured a scrambled egg mixture into the greasy pan.

Freddie made a face.

The eggs started to sizzle and brown and smell.

"It's the way Opa likes them," I told her. "And so do I." Actually, I thought it was a little gross, but it was the way Opa liked them.

Freddie made a choking noise, then began to open and close cabinets and drawers.

"What are you doing?" I asked, finally.

She turned to look at me. "I'm living here now. I need to know where stuff is, don't I? And I need to eat."

I kept my focus on the coagulating eggs and watched Freddie without making it look like I was watching her.

She kept pulling out foodstuffs and making disapproving noises. The cereal wasn't good. The cheese was bad. So were the cold cuts. And the vegetables weren't fresh enough. Finally, she found a box of frozen corn buried beneath some creamed spinach. This she tossed into the microwave.

"You can do that? Frozen foods? Microwave?" I asked as she sat down with a glass of ice water. "Being vegan and all?"

"We're not Amish," she replied. Her next comment was directed at Opa. "Can we *please* go grocery shopping sometime and pick up some stuff I can eat?"

After breakfast, Opa herded Hans-Peter and me into his old VW Beetle and took us down to the deli.

Before my parents and I moved down to Texas, we used to hang out around the place all the time. Delicatessen Kowalski was a couple miles from the house, in this quaint shopping area called Little Swabia and filled with all kinds German American shops, restaurants, *biergartens,* and other places celebrating Teutonic culture and fatty foods.

The deli was narrow but long. Wine, beer, confections, and gifts from central and eastern Europe were displayed in the front part. Opa claimed that the deli also had Chicago's biggest selection of cuckoo clocks, Polish crystal, and beer steins. A glass meat counter along three walls was positioned at the back. Behind it was the butcher shop and sausage works.

The entire place smelled of spice and smoked and congealed animal flesh. It was nauseating.

It didn't help when Hans-Peter hauled out this rack of sausages and began to slice one up on the counter.

"This is a test. I'm trying out a new recipe for the Wurstfest contest," he said. "Spicy smoked bologna. Want to try?"

Before I could formulate a severe enough response, Shohei O'Leary, of all people, swaggered into the store. Shohei was a classmate of mine at the Peshtigo School and was widely regarded as being popular, cute, and, well, kind of an airhead.

Shohei was studying a clipboard. "Oh, hi, Hans-Peter," he said, looking up. "I'm here as your application liaison, and — Freddie? What are you doing here?"

"Shohei," Hans-Peter said, with a nod.

"Wait," I said. "How do you know each other?"

Shohei pulled up short a moment. "My mom took a sushi-making class from his last year," he said. "Why are you here?"

"Hans-Peter is my cousin," I said.

"*Cousin?*" Shohei asked, like the word was new to him.

"My father and his mother are brother and sister," I said. "So, cousins."

"Oh," he said.

"Why are you an application liaison?" I asked him. Working for school administration was a completely not-Shohei thing to do.

He frowned. "My parents made me, since I've been forbidden to do the science fair and —"

"Ahem," Hans-Peter interrupted. "What's an 'application liaison'?"

"Oh, it's new," Shohei replied. "I guess the admission board was concerned about retention rates . . . and, so, that's why I'm here."

Shohei paused like he was expecting Hans-Peter to say something.

Hans-Peter was silent.

"Okay," Shohei continued, lifting a page off the clipboard, "says here you like dinosaurs."

"Yeah?" Hans-Peter said, somewhat defensively.

"Great," Shohei replied. "How'd you like to meet Dr. Lee?"

"*The* Dr. Lee?" Hans-Peter asked. "Dr. *Julia* Lee? Sure!"

"Good," Shohei said, looking at some notes. "I'm supposed to arrange things and you can get a tour of the catacombs, if you want."

"Who's Dr. Lee?" I asked.

"Dr. Julia Lee," Hans-Peter said, clearly pained at having to relieve my ignorance, "is one of the world's foremost therapod experts."

I must have looked blank, because Hans-Peter supplied, "*T. rex. Carnotaurus. Allosaurus. Utahraptor.* Pretty much all your really cool carnivores. She also runs the Peshtigo School Montana Excavation Program."

Shohei handed Hans-Peter some brochures. "This explains everything," he said. "I'll set up the date and get back to you. Gotta go." Then he snatched up one of the bologna samples and popped it into his mouth. A second later, red-faced, he started coughing. "Water!" he sputtered.

"Too spicy?" Hans-Peter asked, handing him a bottle of water from the cooler.

"No, it's great," Shohei replied, eyes watering, coughing again. "But I thought Germans liked *bland* food."

Hans-Peter made a note in his sausage journal.

At this point, I was tempted to head off, but it occurred to me that Shohei might be useful. I said to him, "You wouldn't happen to have time to help our cause?"

He looked at me like space aliens had just landed on my head.

"The Union of Students Concerned About Cruelty to Animals," I clarified, willing my face not to turn red. "We're building a float for homecoming. Maybe you could give us a hand?"

Nothing.

"Well, think about it," I said.

Hans-Peter

Because Freddie spent most of the day at the deli complaining about a lack of food choices, Opa drove us to the supermarket immediately after we closed up.

He parked the Beetle out front under a light in the parking lot and handed me some money and a list. "Buy these things," he said. "And I expect change back." Then he sat back and began to work on his crossword puzzle.

Freddie and I climbed out of the car and each grabbed a shopping cart.

"I've got my own list," Freddie said. "Meet you at checkout." With that, she headed off toward the vegetables.

For a while, I just went up and down the aisles, paying attention to what I was buying — dairy, breakfast cereal, mac and cheese, and other American food that Opa doesn't sell at the deli or doesn't get wholesale.

Then I heard Freddie's voice the next aisle over. "You

know," she was saying, "dolphin-safe is still fish-dangerous. It still involves killing. Just because tuna are not as cute as dolphins doesn't mean they deserve pain and death."

I was tempted to skip that aisle, but tuna was on my list. I wheeled my cart around to where Freddie was talking to a woman with a wide-eyed toddler in the cart. Freddie's cart had only a few things in it. Soy milk and three packages of tofu.

"Could we just shop?" I asked Freddie.

As Freddie turned to me, the lady touched her on the arm. "That was fascinating," she said. "Thank you." Then she wheeled her cart around and fled.

"See, she didn't mind," Freddie said.

"Maybe," I said. "But she took the tuna."

Freddie sniffed and marched off with her own cart.

I quickly finished up. When I was done, I pushed my cart to checkout. Freddie wasn't there yet. She couldn't have that much on her list, I thought, so I decided to go find her. I figured she was probably lecturing more folks on the immorality of their diets.

I wheeled my cart down to the back of the store and spotted Freddie over by where produce ended and seafood began. Her cart was a lot more full than it had been. She was standing in front of the lady handing out samples of the crab dip.

I reached them in time to hear Freddie ask, "How would you like it if someone tore off one of your limbs and mixed it up with some mayonnaise and put it on a cracker?"

I could tell this made the samples lady uncomfortable.

"They grow back," I told Freddie.

"What?" she asked.

"Crabs," I said. "Their claws. They grow back. And they really don't have that advanced a nervous system, so they probably can't feel much."

"It still involves mutilation," Freddie replied, "and people probably use the rest of the crab, too. Don't they?" The last was directed at the samples lady. "*Don't* they?"

The lady's mouth moved, but no sounds came out.

"Excuse me," came another voice. A man had walked up behind us. "Are you the young lady who's harassing our customers?" According to his name tag, his name was Bill, and he was the store manager. "Alice, you can leave," he told the lady.

"I am not harassing your customers," my cousin said while Alice scooted around her. Freddie drew herself up. "I am exercising my First Amendment right to explain the consequences of living a life built on the suffering of and grievous bodily harm to other sentient creatures."

"Uh-huh," Bill answered. He tapped his foot. "I'm afraid I'm going to have to ask you to leave." He moved as if to take her by the arm.

"You can't do that!" Freddie protested, twisting out of his way.

Bill glared. "I could call the police."

"You'd better go," I told Freddie, hoping she would take the hint.

"Do you know this girl?" Bill asked me.

There was only one thing I could say to make sure I got out of there with any groceries at all. "Never seen her before in my life."

"What?!" Freddie exclaimed.

Before she could continue, I went on. "She just came up to me in frozen foods and started saying crazy things. Said I reminded her of her cousin, too." I shook my head in mock sadness. "Miss," I told her, "you'd better leave."

Freddie was too stunned, or maybe angry, to say anything further to me. She remained silent as she let Bill escort her back to the front of the store.

Freddie

As soon as I escaped from the fascist grocer, I headed back to the car, yanked the door open, landed on the seat next to Opa, and slammed the door shut.

"Don't slam the door," Opa said without looking up from his crossword puzzle.

I said nothing.

After a minute, he peered around outside the car. "Where are your groceries?" he asked. "Where is Hans-

Peter?" He put down his crossword puzzle and took off his glasses. "What did you do?"

"I didn't do anything," I replied, crossing my arms.

"No?"

"I was just talking to the samples lady about veganism, and the manager threw me out."

"You were just 'talking' to the samples lady?" Opa asked.

"And one or two other people," I admitted. "And then Hans-Peter tells the manager I'm some kind of crazy person!"

As if he knew we were talking about him, Hans-Peter chose that moment to arrive with the groceries.

I jumped out of the car as he began putting them in the trunk.

"What did you think you were doing?" I demanded. "'I've never met her before . . .'"

He paused, a hand on a grocery bag. "I figured it was the only way we wouldn't *both* get thrown out," he replied, then hefted the bag into the trunk. "*And,* I grabbed your stuff after you were hauled off."

This stopped me. It was slightly clever of him. "You got my groceries?"

"You're welcome," he replied with a slight smirk.

"Thank you," I said, because I didn't want to give him the satisfaction of being able to say I hadn't. "But I am *not* crazy."

"That's what all the crazy people think," he replied, slamming the trunk shut.

"There is nothing crazy about being vegan," I told him, and then went on, in response to his smug look, "How can people be expected to treat other people okay if they don't treat those who most need to be treated okay okay?"

"*What?*"

"Never mind," I said. I could explain later.

Opa started the car as soon as we got in and then apparently decided to ignore the fact that Hans-Peter and I had been arguing and now weren't speaking to each other. "So," he said, "what is a nine letter word for 'tergiversation'?"

Chapter 3

Food Fight

Freddie

My first day back at the Peshtigo School was a challenging one.

I was testing out my new locker combination when Mr. Harrell, the Peshtigo School Vice-Principal and Dean of Student Conduct, appeared at my side.

"Ms. Murchison-Kowalski, please come with me," he said.

I followed him around the Atrium Garden, up to his office. He sat back heavily in his oak office chair while I sat down in one of the high-back chairs in front of him. I waited for him to speak. He was usually filled with all kinds of blather about being a good member of "the Peshtigo School family."

"Ms. Murchison-Kowalski," he began as he grabbed a file in front of him, "we are watching you."

"I haven't done anything," I protested.

"Not today," Mr. Harrell agreed. He tapped the file. "But last year alone, you were brought before student court for the chicken-fried steak incident, and subject to disciplinary action for your conduct at the science fair. And you were only here half a year."

I yawned.

"If I'm boring you —"

"No," I said, sitting up straighter. "I'm sorry. I haven't been getting enough sleep. My cousin's frogs have been loud at night."

"Frogs," he said, drumming his fingers. "Perhaps it's the sign of a guilty conscience."

I didn't say anything.

"Now, where was I?" he asked.

"Student court, half a year," I said.

"Yes," he agreed. "Two grave matters here last year, and now this . . . incident at the football stadium in Texas."

"It was a protest," I said.

Mr. Harrell put down the file and folded his hands on the desk. "Ms. Murchison-Kowalski, you are on probation. Your re-admittance here was not without controversy. If you are seen with anything remotely resembling combustibles, you will be expelled. Is that clear?"

"It is," I replied, somewhat deflated.

"Good," he said. "You are dismissed."

Later, in the school cafeteria lunch line, I ran into Eleanor Mancini, who had been one of the founders of the Union of Students Concerned About Cruelty to Animals.

"I'm glad you're back," she said, clutching her tray of wilted salad and overcooked broccoli. She glanced around, as if trying not to be overheard. "Patrick and Doris have pretty much taken over the executive committee . . . and they refuse to do anything that would upset the administration."

"Oh?" I asked while I paid for my own salad. This was a cause for concern.

We'd founded the Union a couple years back because of the science fair's animal behavioral experiments.

We'd set up this very sophisticated, non-hierarchical organizational structure for our work, since we didn't want anyone to feel as if his or her voice was unimportant. Therefore, everyone who wanted to be was on the executive committee.

In practice, the membership had done what I told them.

Patrick Jarndyce and Doris Witkowski had been members from early on. They had almost always objected to any kind of effective protest because, they claimed, controversy wouldn't help our cause. Patrick Jarndyce, though, just happened to have a father who spent a lot of time at the school, because he was one of our class's volunteer lawyers. (They were sort of like room mothers, but they made you sign a release before they gave you cookies.) I always suspected Patrick's real objective was to avoid doing anything that would upset his father. Or potential clients.

"Let's talk about this," I said as we made our way to an open table. We spent the rest of lunch trying to plan — I hadn't counted on having to persuade anyone about doing the homecoming float. We did manage to canvass a couple of the other members of the executive committee, but by the time of the after-school kickoff meeting, nothing was certain.

The executive committee met in one of the conference rooms off the library. The room would've had a view north toward Oak Street Beach, but there was a new high-rise condominium in the way. I got in early and managed to get seated strategically at the head of the conference table. The members came in and sat down in ones and twos. On my left were Barbara Lee, Marcus Cabrillo, and Doris Witkowski. To my right were Eleanor

Mancini, Susan Caperson, and a new girl whose name was Shawna.

Patrick Jarndyce was the last to arrive, and he did not look happy to see me sitting at the head of the table. All he said was "Hello," though, and then sat next to Doris.

"Thank you for coming," I said, calling the meeting to order. "I thought this year we should work on maintaining our high profile while reaching out to increase our numbers."

There were nods and mutterings of agreement, which was not surprising because I hadn't actually said anything either controversial or meaningful yet.

"So," I continued, "I think we should enter a float in the homecoming parade."

A moment of silence followed.

"You've got to be kidding," Patrick said quietly, but loud enough that it was clear he meant to be heard.

"You have an opinion?" I asked.

"I do," he said, then held up a hand and began ticking off points on his fingers. "One, we've never done a float before. Two, none of us likes football. Three, the *chess* tournament finals usually draw a bigger crowd than homecoming. Four —"

"That was only last year because they had that Russian Grand Master What's-His-Name as a guest judge," Eleanor interrupted.

"Four," Patrick continued, ignoring her, "we could probably do more to increase membership by setting up a table at Prospective Students Day, and, five, does anyone here even know which end of a hammer to pick up?"

"To do what with?" someone asked. Someone else snickered, but this otherwise went over about as well as one of my grandfather's jokes.

Around the table, there were enough nodding heads that I probably couldn't reject Patrick's objections outright.

"How hard could it be?" I asked, trying to sound ingenuous. "And I like the idea of a table at Prospective Students Day. Surely we can do both?"

"Sounds like a good idea to me," Susan said, on cue. "Our participation might help the administration think of us as a more mainstream organization."

"Then we're agreed?" I asked.

They all nodded, this time in my favor.

"Great," I said, relieved, and resolving to keep an eye on Patrick. "Anything else?"

"I would like something done about Ms. Wilson," Barbara said. "According to her syllabus, she does electricity experiments on animals."

"Just the limbs," Patrick said. "Not the entire animal. And they're not alive at the time."

"Once dismembered is twice dead," Shawna piped up.

"I agree," I said, feeling magnanimous. "Let's make this an action item."

Hans-Peter

My first day of eighth grade back at my regular old neighborhood school, I went to see my math teacher from last year.

"Ms. Sutherland?" I began, walking up to her desk.

"What can I do for you?" she asked, looking up from some papers. "Are you going to join the math team?"

I shook my head. "I don't like to take tests." Taking them in class was bad enough. I had no intention of doing anything that involved taking them recreationally.

"I know," she said. "What brings you here?"

"I'm applying for admission to the Peshtigo School, and I was wondering if you'd be willing to recommend me," I told her. "There's kind of an early deadline." The Peshtigo School had what they called an "accelerated admissions" procedure.

She smiled. "Peshtigo? I'd be happy to. And I'll get to it right away."

I handed her the Peshtigo recommendation form, then hesitated.

"Is there something else?"

"When do you need Euclid and Pythagoras back?"

"Why don't you keep them?" she said with a sigh. "They're going to be enforcing the rule against classroom pets, so I'm not going to be able to take them here."

"Really?" I asked. This was fantastic. "Thanks!"

That night, Opa released Freddie and me from deli duty early — me so I could get to work on my Peshtigo application essays, and her because she was supposed to be cooking that night. I wasn't looking forward to bark and twigs, though, so I'd made sure to eat a large lunch.

With Freddie safely upstairs in the kitchen, I grabbed a jacket and went down to the basement, where my computer had been exiled, wedged in beside the dinosaur head. Opa and I had set up the desk under a bare bulb next to Rex, which really did take up almost too much room. We'd managed to clean the place up a bit when we'd moved the computer down, but the main room still had bare walls with peeling gray paint, dirty windows, some built-in cabinets, a wash basin, and a washer and dryer. There was also a semi-finished half bathroom, with a toilet that had no seat and a sink that had only cold water and that you had to let run for a while to clean out the rust. Opa had been meaning to put in a new shower, but hadn't gotten to it yet. The only other room, behind the stairs, was Opa's workshop, where he stored power tools and hardware that were rarely, if ever, used.

Most of the Peshtigo School application was standard stuff. Name, date of birth, address, grades, test scores, extracurricular activities. List of recommenders. The essays, though, were tough, where they said "the Admissions Committee can learn what special contributions each candidate will be able to make to the Peshtigo School family."

I wrote an e-mail to my mom, but hadn't gotten anywhere on the essays when the kitchen smoke alarm sounded.

I waited a moment, but when it didn't turn off I ran up the stairs to see what was going on. At the top, I nearly tripped over Baschi, Opa's cat, who dashed through the cat entry in the basement door to escape the noise. Flinging open the door, I froze briefly as my eyes started to water. The air was filled with smoke, and there was an inferno on the stove. Freddie was trying to open the window over the kitchen sink.

"What are you doing?" I yelled.

"Where's a fire extinguisher?" she yelled right back.

I pushed her aside and pulled it out from under the sink. Making sure the burner was off, I let loose with the foam, coating the stovetop and tile backsplash.

When the flames were out, I said, "Are you okay?"

Freddie's face was a little sooty. "I'm fine," she replied, staring at the foamy wreckage. "But thanks."

"What happened?" I asked, opening the back door in hopes that the smoke would clear out quickly.

"Blackened tofu," Freddie replied, running the back of her hand across her forehead.

"That's for sure," I said with a slight grin. "You might want to wash your face."

She gave me a sour look, but went. The smoke alarm finally turned off as she closed the bathroom door. When she came back, her face was cleaner. "Cooking," she said, "is not as easy as it looks. When does Opa get home?"

"You have about an hour," I told her.

She put on an oven mitt, then grabbed the sauté pan and tossed it into the sink. Turning to me, she said, "I'll give you some pointers on your Peshtigo essays if you promise not to tell Opa."

Was she kidding? "Deal."

"Write about sausage," she said. "No one else will."

Hans-Peter

PESHTIGO SCHOOL APPLICATION ESSAY NO. 1.
Write about something you do for fun.

Sausage. Kielbasa. Wurst. Whatever you call it, it's the food of Odysseus. The ancient Babylonians. The Roman legions. And Chicago, Illinois.

Please note that this essay is not for the squeamish.

The secret to good smoked bratwurst is fresh ingredients. This point cannot be overemphasized.

Thus, the first step in making a good bratwurst is to kill a pig. (If your recipe calls for veal, as well, you will also need to kill a juvenile cow.) If you do not have access to livestock on the hoof or do not feel inclined to slaughter them yourself, you may obtain the ingredients (pork, pork fat, and veal) from any competent butcher.

Start with about 2 pounds of pork shoulder meat, ½ pound of pork back fat, and ½ pound of veal shoulder. (If you don't want to use veal, you can use beef or simply an additional ½ pound of pork.)

The meat must be ground and mixed with seasonings of choice. These typically include various combinations of salt, pepper, mustard seed, garlic, mace, sage, nutmeg, allspice, caraway seeds, marjoram. Do not overmix, because this will melt the fat.

While mixing, prepare the casings. Edible casings are usually made from hog intestines. To prepare the casings, rinse off the salt and soak briefly in a very dilute mixture of vinegar and water. Then briefly drip dry.

Once the mixing and casing preparation have been completed, the casings must be stuffed. This can be accomplished by hand or through use of a device known as a stuffer. A stuffer essentially has one opening with a press for feeding the meat mixture into and another, funnel-shaped opening to which the casing is attached. The exiting mixture is fed into the casing.

To stuff: Attach an open end of the casing to the exit funnel and slowly feed the meat mixture into the top of the device. Twist when filled to about 4–5 inches full to form the links. Use a sharp knife to cut the links apart.

The raw brats can then be refrigerated for up to two days and then cooked before eating to an internal temperature of about 160° Fahrenheit. Alternatively, the brats can be hot- or cold-smoked to the same temperature.

Safety note: Make sure all surfaces and utensils are clean, and do not taste the raw pork mixture. The presence of *Trichinella* worm larvae can lead to trichinosis, which can cause severe pain, abdominal discomfort, and death.

Chapter 4

The Frogs

Freddie

I am not a thief. Or a kidnapper. I blame the whole thing on weeks of losing sleep caused by loud amphibians and the absence of sufficient lavatory resources in the standard Chicago-style bungalow.

Back in Texas, my house had a bathroom, complete with soaking tub, for each of the bedrooms, plus two extra half baths just for non-overnight guests. Here, though, the three main floor bedrooms shared a single bath, which Hans-Peter occupied an extraordinary amount of the time. Especially in the mornings.

I pounded on the bathroom door. "Would you hurry up in there?" I said. "And don't steal my shampoo again!"

"I'll be done in a minute," Hans-Peter replied.

I leaned my head against the door. At least the shower had stopped. Now I heard the sink faucet. "What takes you so long?" I asked. "I'm the one with all the hair! And I don't even blow-dry it!"

He opened the door, applying toothpaste to his brush, wearing his usual early morning soccer shorts and T-shirt. "Ten minutes for shower. Five minutes for brushing teeth and hair. It doesn't take me any longer than you. I just manage to get in here first." He closed the door. "If you're in a hurry, go downstairs."

"There's no hot water!" I exclaimed. "Or shower, for that matter!"

Hans-Peter didn't answer. The door to his bedroom was open. I walked up to the frog tank. Pythagoras and Euclid were sitting there on the little gray stone, looking like perfectly contented frogs being held captive against their will. And they were quiet.

As a vegan, of course, it would be improper for me to harm them, but they didn't know that. "You better watch yourselves," I said.

With that, Opa's attic door opened. He was already dressed for work.

"Morning, Opa, can I use your bathroom? Hans-Peter's hogging the one down here again!"

"I'm done," Hans-Peter said, opening the bathroom door. "It's all yours. And I was *not* hogging it!"

Opa pointed at me. "You," he said. "Go to the bathroom." Then he pointed at Hans-Peter. "You. Get dressed. You look like a bum."

Opa and Hans-Peter took off before Eleanor Mancini and her brother — my ride to the Peshtigo School — arrived. Home alone, I went back into Hans-Peter's room and took another look at the very loud frogs.

"I'm going to set you free," I told them.

When Eleanor and her brother got there, I had them help me take the tank from Hans-Peter's room and load it into the back of their pickup. I briefly considered taking Euclid and Pythagoras down to the river, but that would be cruel. If the rats — which in Chicago are the size of small ponies — didn't get them, the winter probably would.

So I took them to school instead.

It was not a great day at Delicatessen Kowalski. Of course, most days were not great days. True, Opa didn't make me work in the butcher shop handling entrails, but even up front with Mrs. Fraunhofer, doing checkout and generally keeping the place in order, you couldn't get away from the *smell*.

It wasn't like anything was obviously decomposing — Opa kept the place so amazingly clean that bacteria and parasites were probably terrified to come within miles. It was just that, no matter where you were, you couldn't get away from the idea that the whole place was dedicated to delivering dismembered, disemboweled, and mutilated fauna, all wrapped up in freezer-safe, butcher-quality wax paper.

Every now and then, though, you came face-to-face with it. Like that afternoon, when the irate baby-boomer yuppie woman wearing a severe charcoal suit and carrying a package of butcher paper walked in and held a slice of ham in front of my face. "Look at this!" she demanded.

"It looks like ham," I told her, wondering why on Earth anyone would be bringing ham *into* a deli. "We sell thirty-seven different kinds." I was not necessarily proud of this, but it seemed the appropriate thing to say.

"Are you trying to be funny?" the lady asked.

"Not about animal flesh," I assured her. Despite myself, I studied the sample she held out. It didn't seem rancid and it looked reasonably hamlike. I did not touch it. "What seems to be the problem?"

"It's sliced too thin," she said, in a disgusted tone.

I stared at her, trying to figure out if she was serious. "Oh," I said, glancing around for Mrs. Fraunhofer, who wasn't in sight. "Maybe you could layer the slices?"

"Listen, young lady," the yuppie said, "I don't know who you are, but I have been coming here for some time, and I have to say, the quality of both the food and the staff have been declining for years."

Before I could reply, the cuckoo clock went off, giving me a chance to decide what to say. I chose to be polite.

"Hypertension and hysteria," I said, "are well-known to be caused by too much animal protein. Also heart attacks. Maybe you should consider converting to veganism."

The lady looked like one of her cholesterol-clogged arteries was ready to burst. Before that happened, though, Hans-Peter emerged from the storeroom carrying a case of *spaetzl* mix.

"Mrs. Bishop," he said soothingly, "was there a problem with your order?"

Mrs. Bishop gave me a cold look, then replied to Hans-Peter. "This is the third time this month the ham has been sliced too thin."

Hans-Peter didn't miss a beat. "I'm very sorry," he said. "We've been having problems with one of the slicing machines. It won't happen again." Then he led her to the back deli case.

While Opa was dealing with her, Hans-Peter returned to the checkout counter. "Look," he said, "when a customer has a complaint, just nod politely and make it right."

"But she's insane!" I told him.

"Yes," Hans-Peter replied. "But she spends a lot of money here, and if she wants her ham sliced thick, it's the way she should get it."

Hans-Peter

When I got home, I went to feed, water, and generally check on Euclid and Pythagoras, like I usually did. They were gone. Gone. Gone!

"Freddie!" I yelled. "Freddie! Where are my frogs?"

As I entered the kitchen, Opa paused, hand on the refrigerator door.

"Euclid and Pythagoras are missing," I told him.

"Did the cat get them?" Opa asked, frowning. "They are not poisonous?"

"The tank's missing, too," I said. Then I pounded on Freddie's closed door. "Freddie! Where are my frogs?"

"It is inappropriate to talk of owning another sentient creature," Freddie said, opening her door. "They are not *your* frogs."

"What did you do with them?" I asked.

"They're not here," Freddie replied. "They're in a better place."

"You *killed* them?" I asked, astonished.

"I did not kill them," Freddie replied, like the thief was insulted I'd imply she was a murderer, too.

That could only mean one thing, which was almost as bad. "You let them loose? Where?"

"They're not loose," Freddie said. It was like she was

discussing the weather. "I took them someplace a lot safer and more comfortable —"

"Opa!" I said, glancing at him, demanding intervention.

Opa pulled a chair from the kitchen table and sat. "Where are the frogs?"

She hesitated. "They're a lot better off than where they were."

"Frederika!" Opa raised his voice.

"I'm not saying," Freddie replied. "You'd only make me bring them back."

"So," Opa said, "you have now lost your Internet privileges for one month. Shall we try for your cell phone as well?"

Freddie went back to her room and returned, handing Opa the phone.

"Very well," Opa said. "Three months, no Internet. Three months, no cell phone. You will also pay for the tanks and the frogs and whatever else you took. Now go to your room."

"Is that it?" I asked as the door slammed behind Freddie. I thought Opa would do something more, well, effective. Euclid and Pythagoras were still missing.

"The frogs are much better off at the Peshtigo School," he replied quietly.

"How do you know that's where they are?" I asked.

"Where else would they be?"

"And you're not going to make her bring them back?" The whole thing was completely unfair. The frogs had been *mine*.

"They were," Opa said, "loud. And they were supposed to be going back to your school anyway."

"How would you like it if I took Baschi to the Peshtigo School?" I asked.

"Enough!" Opa said, pounding the table. "Frogs are not pets. They are things the French eat."

I didn't reply. It was always a bad sign when Opa invoked something the French ate. I wasn't going to get any further with him.

It *was* totally unfair. He let Freddie get away with . . . almost as much as they let her get away with at the Peshtigo School. What was it with her anyway?

I went to my room and very carefully didn't slam the door. I was still mad, though. She'd come into my room and stolen my frogs, and Opa wasn't doing anything about it! I dropped onto my bed and stared at the empty place on my shelf.

Freddie

A couple weeks later, in history class, Mrs. Parker was discussing the Defenestration of Prague and I was writing a letter to my parents when I was called out to go see Vice-Principal Harrell. I grabbed my books and USCACA file and followed the messenger.

When I got to Mr. Harrell's office, he was at his desk and James Jarndyce, Esq., father of Patrick Jarndyce, was seated in one of the conference chairs.

I took the other. "You wanted to see me?"

"Thank you for coming," Mr. Harrell said, folding his hands. "We hear you're planning to enter a float into this year's homecoming parade."

"You 'hear'?" I asked, glancing at Mr. Jarndyce. I could guess from whom.

"Yes," Mr. Harrell continued, "and we would like to urge you not to."

"Urge me not to?" I asked. "Why?" I thought I knew, and I was not going to make it easy for them.

"Rumor has it," Mr. Jarndyce said, "that you're planning a dramatic halftime statement . . . and that, coupled with your history of destroying football-related school property, has us concerned."

"I would never listen to rumor," I said.

"Certain members of your organization," Mr. Jarndyce continued smoothly, "are concerned that any extreme behavior could adversely affect their academic futures."

Definitely Patrick. The wimp. He hadn't said anything during our second meeting when we'd decided on the float design. Obviously, though, he was unhappy that I was in charge again, but I'd thought he'd confine himself to arguments and snide comments during the executive committee meetings. Having his father go to Mr. Harrell, on the other hand, was sneaky and underhanded.

I should've expected it.

"We also have the alumni to think about," Mr. Harrell said. "They tend not to like bad publicity."

As he was talking, I realized why I was there. My experience at having been a defendant six times in Student Court had taught me something — they couldn't prevent a chartered student organization from participating in school functions.

Because I knew they couldn't stop me, I decided to try being reasonable.

"Can I show you something?" I asked. I pulled the file out of my backpack and placed some design sheets onto Mr. Harrell's desk. "This is all we're doing. We're calling it 'Poseidon's Revenge.'"

"You're building a skiing porcupine?" Mr. Harrell asked.

"It's a blowfish," I said. I'd gotten the idea from Aunt Johanna, the blowfish chef.

"Why does it need skis?" he asked.

"Those are *sharks*," I replied. "The theme is death rising from the oceans. The seas fight back. That sort of thing."

"Oh," he said.

I didn't tell him the best part. That we were going to make it a functioning blowfish — it would inflate and deflate on command.

"This is beside the point," Mr. Jarndyce said in a condescending tone.

"No," Mr. Harrell said. "Jim, it's all right." He looked at me. "As long as this is what you do, it's fine."

"It is," I assured him.

Back at the deli after school, Hans-Peter was restocking.

I handed him the design sketch.

"How do I build this?" I asked, setting down the paper in front of him. "I want the blowfish to be able to puff up like in real life."

"How would I know?" he replied.

My cousin seems smart, but sometimes I wonder.

"Oh, I don't know," I said. "How did you make the really big dinosaur head you keep at home in the basement?"

Hans-Peter leaned against the shelves. "Will my giving you an answer make you go away faster?"

"Yes," I told him decisively. "And I'll be happy to do so."

"It won't work," he said, handing me the sheet. "Bye."

"What do you mean?" I planted my feet and glared.

"Let me put it like this," he said. "Let's see . . . what

was that little thing you did? Let me give you a hint: Ribbit-ribbit!"

I couldn't believe he was still holding that against me. Well, come to think of it, I could, but I wasn't going to let him. "Look," I said. "I am not going to apologize for the frogs. They're safe."

"I'm not going to let you get away with that," he said. "Frog-napper."

"Yeah, fine, go ahead," I replied. I could deal with that when I had to deal with that. For now, though, "Just tell me about the float."

He turned back to the canned goods.

"I'll help you more with your application essays," I told him.

He hesitated.

"Okay," he said, finally, then paused. "The thing in the basement is basically papier-mache over chicken wire. It's essentially completely rigid. You can do that for the sharks, but not the blowfish, if you want it to inflate."

"Are you telling me there is no way I can get it to inflate?" I asked.

"Maybe," Hans-Peter said. "I suppose if you had a compressor and a big balloon or bladder or something, you could make it work."

That made a certain amount of sense, but there was

still a problem. "I see," I said. "And where am I likely to find these?"

"The engineering science surplus store over on Pulaski," Hans-Peter replied. "Now go away."

I did.

Hans-Peter

I was downstairs at the computer working on some English homework when the basement door opened, and Opa yelled down, "Hans-Peter! You have a phone call!"

I logged off and grabbed the basement extension. "Hello?"

"Hi, Hans-Peter, it's me. Shohei."

"What's going on?" I asked. I hadn't really expected to hear from him, although I still wasn't exactly sure what an application liaison did.

"Well, you're not doing anything tomorrow, are you?" he said.

"Why?" I asked.

"You're meeting Dr. Lee at nine o'clock."

"Dr. Lee of the Field Museum?"

"No," he replied. "Dr. Lee of Starfleet Command. Of course, Dr. Lee of the Field Museum."

"*Tomorrow* tomorrow?" I asked. I was not going to panic, I told myself. Just because I didn't have any time at all to prepare myself. What kind of application liaison was he, anyway?

"Yeah, sorry," he said. "Forgot to check the schedule."

When I went to ask Opa if he could drive me to the Field Museum the next day, Freddie was there. "Great!" she said. "I'm going, too!"

"Why?" I asked. I really didn't want her around. The interview was bad enough. I didn't want to have to worry about Freddie running amok.

"Because they're having a display of Rose Parade floats," she said. "I'm doing research for the one I'm building with the USCACA." She went to her room and brought back a brochure.

Opa frowned. "Why would they have a display of parade floats?"

"I don't know," Freddie said. "Anthropology, maybe? Can you drive me?"

"You can't just go some other time?" I asked.

"No," Freddie said, "but don't worry. I'll be leaving you as soon as the car stops. I have no desire to spend the day with you and Shohei and some weird lady in a glorified animal morgue and taxidermy freak show."

I probably shouldn't have executed my plan to get back at Freddie the morning I had to be somewhere at nine o'clock. But isn't the entire point of a practical joke/revenge plot the springing of it when the victim least expects it? And, besides, she took my frogs.

It wasn't even that difficult. It took all of five minutes, maybe six.

"All yours," I told her as I was leaving the bathroom.

I went out to the kitchen, where Opa was having his morning coffee and doing his crossword puzzle. I poured myself some cereal and had just sat down to eat it when the bathroom door was flung open and an irate and damp Freddie stormed out of the bathroom.

"What did you put in my shampoo?" she demanded, hands on her black bathrobe sash.

"What makes you think I'd put anything in your shampoo?" I asked, possibly too innocently.

She answered by grabbing my cereal bowl and pouring the whole thing, milk and all, over my head.

As I jumped up to grab the towel that hung from the refrigerator handle, Opa protested. "Frederika!" he said. "What are you doing?"

She glared at him, then replied. "He put *honey* in my vegan shampoo."

When Opa looked over at me, I made sure to stay silent and tried to look injured. "I see," Opa said, folding his newspaper. "Are you sure that the things in your shampoo simply did not congeal on their own?"

"It's *honey*!" she insisted. "Made from real bee vomit! Smell it!" She walked over and held out her hair.

He sniffed, then nodded. "*Ja*, it is honey," he said. Then his nose twitched. "But why do you also smell like chicken soup?"

Freddie growled and glared at me.

"What makes you think I did it?" I asked. "I'm allergic to bees."

"What did you do, and why did you do it?" Opa replied.

"She stole my frogs," I said, "and they're not coming back anytime soon."

There was a pause while Freddie ground her teeth.

"That is a reason," Opa acknowledged. "Not a good one, but it is a reason. Now, *what* did you do?"

"Honey in the shampoo," I said. "Chicken bouillon cubes in the shower head."

"I see," he said, sipping his coffee. Opa looked thoughtful for a moment. "You did not scratch the finish on the showerhead when you took it off?"

"No," I replied. "I used a towel under the pipe wrench."

"Well, that at least was not stupid," he said. "Frederika, why don't you let the shower run for a few minutes to clean it out, and then you can finish and get ready."

"I don't have any more vegan shampoo," she said through clenched teeth.

"Then Hans-Peter will get you some from the corner store," he told her.

"But, but . . . ," I protested, doing the time calculation. I was supposed to be at the Field Museum in less than an hour. He couldn't be serious. "We'll be late!"

Opa shook his head. "*I* will not be late. *You* will be late."

"But —"

"The longer you sit here, the later you will be."

I ran, milk still dripping.

Chapter 5

The Dinosaurs of Dr. Lee

Hans-Peter

I couldn't *believe* Opa made me late for my interview with Dr. Lee just for pulling a minor joke on Freddie, especially when he hadn't done a thing to get Euclid and Pythagoras back. It was totally unjust.

When Opa pulled up and let Freddie and me out, Shohei was sitting on the museum steps. "You're late!" he said.

"I know," I replied, climbing the stairs and not willing to go into any great detail on why. "Can we still get in to see Dr. Lee?"

Shohei and I entered the main hall, Freddie a couple steps behind and off to one side, trying to look like she was only coincidentally going in the same direction.

"Dr. Lee said she had a meeting but maybe could make time when it's over," Shohei replied. He walked over to the courtesy phone at the guard desk. "Hi, could you let Dr. Lee know her nine o'clock is here? Thanks."

"She said she'd meet us over at the Sue display," Shohei said.

"Did she say when?" I asked, looking at my watch.

He shook his head as we crossed the Main Hall to the *T. rex* and entrance to the permanent dinosaur exhibit. Freddie left us halfway there to check out the parade floats.

An hour later, we were still waiting for Dr. Lee when Freddie wandered back over. "Nice dinosaur," she said. "How much longer are we going to be here?"

Shohei shrugged.

"This place creeps me out," Freddie added, crossing her arms. "I don't like —"

I interrupted because I was a little on edge and because I wasn't in the mood to listen to her lecture. "I already know you don't like the display of dead animals," I told her. "This is exactly why I didn't want you here. Do you think you could put the whole kooky vegan business on hold for a while?"

"I was going to say," she replied, "that I don't like mummies."

"Oh," Shohei said, "then you should probably stay out of the stairwell. They've got a sliced human body over there." He looked puzzled. "Or is that over at the Museum of Science and Industry?"

"It's at Science and Industry," came a voice that did not sound happy. An Asian woman about Freddie's height, wearing glasses and scowling, came up to us. "I'm Dr. Lee."

I wondered how much she'd heard.

"You, I know," she said, pointing at Shohei. "You, I have heard about," she addressed Freddie. Then she looked at me. "That means you must be Hans-Peter, who apparently cannot tell time and who is bigoted against vegans."

"Ummm . . ." I realized with horror that Dr. Lee herself might be vegan.

"Since it is now noon, and because we do not ever 'put that vegan thing on hold,' I will meet you here at one." She gave me a look. "That's when the big hand is on the twelve and the little hand is on the one." Dr. Lee gestured at Freddie. "Ms. Murchison-Kowalski, would you care to join me for lunch?" As they headed off, Dr. Lee glanced back and repeated. "One o'clock."

When they were out of earshot, I groaned. I should just leave. Nothing good could come of this interview.

"It wasn't that bad," Shohei said.

I groaned again. "Are all Peshtigo School faculty that . . . that . . ."

He looked thoughtful. "She's an adjunct. Regular faculty are worse. Don't worry about it. Let's grab lunch. There's this place here where they have the best cheese fries . . ."

Shohei and I got back early. Freddie and Dr. Lee arrived precisely on time.

"Your cousin tells me you can, in fact, tell time," Dr. Lee said, "and that you are not, and I quote, 'as dumb as you look.' So, say something intelligent."

What had Freddie told her? I wondered, glancing over. She seemed suddenly fascinated with a hangnail.

I took a breath, still pretty much frozen.

"And still he says nothing," Dr. Lee said, pinching the bridge of her nose. "All right, tell me something . . . something I do not know."

"*T. rex* didn't sleep much and couldn't see its arms," I blurted.

She raised an eyebrow. I couldn't tell if it was because she was surprised I had said something smart or the opposite. "Continue," she said.

"Which means the arms were probably vestigial since any kind of manipulation would require a more sophisticated brain than we think it may have had. Maybe. I think."

Dr. Lee's mouth twitched. "I see. And 'didn't sleep much'?"

I started babbling. "Well, their days were shorter — only about fourteen hours — so if they had a circadian rhythm based on a day, they wouldn't sleep much . . ."

"Per day," Dr. Lee said.

"Yeah," I replied, but it was more like a question.

At least she wasn't laughing.

"Let's go," she said. "We have a tour to do."

The whole business at the Field Museum was unnerving. I was never able to get a sense of whether I was making a good impression or just making a fool of myself. Still, I wouldn't even have had that much to go on if Freddie hadn't put in a good word for me at lunch. So, after dinner that night, I went into her room.

"Thanks," I said.

She was on her bed reading a book on organic gardening.

"I guess I owe you one," I added.

"Yes, you do," she replied, putting the book aside. "So I'm going to call in the favor. Right now."

"Explain," I said.

"What do you think of Shohei?" she asked.

I hesitated. "He seems a little disorganized."

She made an exasperated noise. "Do you think he'd make a good member of the USCACA float committee?"

"Oh," I said. "I suppose he could carry things. Why, though? Isn't his favorite food cheese fries?"

"He's popular, and having him participate could inspire some others to join our cause," she replied. "Sort of like a celebrity endorsement. So here's the deal: You get him to help with the float and we're even."

Hmm. "That's a pretty lame reason," I said.

For once, she didn't reply. No lecture. Nothing.

And then I realized the real reason she wanted Shohei there. She'd never admit it to me, though. Never. "All right," I said, "I'll do it."

"Good," she replied, looking fractionally relieved. "And can I say something?"

I paused.

"You're worrying a lot about what Dr. Lee thought of you. The important question is, what did *you* think about *her*?"

I called Shohei immediately because I thought it would be a good idea to get it over with as soon as possible. "Hi," I said.

"What's up?" he replied.

"My cousin wants me to ask you to help her . . . association . . . build their animal rights float for the homecoming parade." I'd decided that straightforward was the best approach. Shohei did not seem like one for subtlety.

"Why?" he asked.

"Why did she ask me to ask you or why does she want you to?"

"Both," he said, which caused me to revise my opinion on his subtlety.

"First," I told him, "I don't know." It was the truth, but I had a couple guesses. "Second, actually, I also don't know." This was also the truth.

"Guess," he said.

He didn't specify as to which question. "She said she thinks," I told him, "that since you're apparently popular, it would benefit their mission to have you join them and that it might inspire others. And 'become one with the cause.'"

"Oh," he replied, sounding vaguely disappointed.

I played the trump card. "There's also a chance she likes you."

He was silent.

Then, "I'll try to make it."

I gave Shohei the time, date, and address, then hung

up and tried not to think about it too much. Shohei and Freddie?

Freddie

It was the Friday night before everyone was scheduled to converge on our garage to start building "Poseidon's Revenge." Opa had parked his VW out front to make room while I made sure we had everything we needed.

We had a plan. We had plywood. We had two-by-fours. We had chicken wire, a rubber inflatable bladder, an air compressor, and a trailer. We had yellow, red, white, black, and blue squares of tissue paper; cardboard, multicolored foil, and yards of bunting. We had gallons of glue. We had wire cutters. We had a circular saw, sawhorses, a nail gun, and an industrial stapler.

We had one problem.

"So," Opa said, returning. "When should I be here?"

"What do you mean?" I asked, as I had visions of bad jokes and *braunschweiger*, neither of which would go over well with the more committed members of USCACA.

"You will need me to be operating the power tools," Opa said, sounding surprised.

"Oh, we can do that," I said, trying for casual. "Don't you have to be at the deli?"

"Always," he replied. "But I am willing to make an exception. Mrs. Fraunhofer and Ernst can handle things tomorrow."

"But, really —"

"While you are here," Opa said, "you are my responsibility. I will absolutely not have you or your friends injuring yourselves on anything that gets its power from an internal combustion engine or Commonwealth Edison. When you are sixteen and have a driver's license, that is soon enough." He paused, waving a finger. "But you will have to pay for your own insurance."

I was completely unable to persuade Opa to be elsewhere Saturday morning. Eleanor was the first to arrive, though, and she didn't seem to have a problem with Opa working the machinery.

"It'll get it done faster," she said. Eleanor can be very practical. Then she paused at the entrance to the living room, gesturing at the rug. "Is that wool?"

"There are limits," I told her, "to what even I can do."

We went out onto the front porch to wait for the rest of the group to arrive. We watched as a black Mercedes sedan with tinted windows pulled up. To our surprise, Patrick Jarndyce got out.

70

As he headed up the sidewalk, I muttered to Eleanor, "What's *he* doing here?" I'd told her about being called in to see Mr. Harrell and his father.

"Probably wants to take the credit if things go well and shift the blame if things go wrong," Eleanor replied.

Patrick came up the walk, grinning. "Hi, ready to build a float?"

Hans-Peter

The doorbell rang at eight o'clock the next morning while Freddie was in the shower. It was Shohei. "Am I too early?" he asked.

"No," I said. I didn't tell him "for yesterday." "You're the first." I paused. "By about four hours."

"Oh," he said.

At that moment, Freddie came out of the bathroom, and walked into the dining room. She was in her black robe and had a towel turban on her head. "Who was at the door?" she asked. Then she spotted Shohei, screamed, and fled.

"Stay here," I told Shohei, then went to check on my cousin.

"Why didn't you tell me someone was here?" she demanded, opening her bedroom door a crack when I knocked. "Take him to the garage."

I went back to the living room. "Her Excellency wants me to take you to the garage."

"I could just come back and —"

I shook my head. "I think she wants to put you to work."

He grabbed his backpack and followed me through the kitchen. "By the way," he said, pulling a Peshtigo School envelope out of the pack. "Here's the date for your alumni-community interview."

I let out a sigh. "How much more is there?"

"Not much," Shohei said. "Interview. School tour. Test. Essays. You're almost there."

"'Almost,' he says," I muttered. "Who's the interview with?"

"I don't know," he replied. "They don't tell us. Supposed to be more objective or something." He glanced at Freddie's door as we passed by. "You'll be getting that info in a couple days."

This sounded unduly mysterious but typical of the Peshtigo School. I was anxious, though, because I didn't think I'd be getting that favorable a review from Dr. Lee.

I led Shohei out to the garage and opened the overhead door. The basic framework had been finished yesterday. It almost looked like it might someday become a real float.

"What am I supposed to do?" he asked, looking at it.

I shrugged. "I don't know. Something with the glue and tissue paper."

That was when Freddie showed up. "Thanks," she said. "I'll take it from here."

Freddie

Hans-Peter was an idiot. How hard would it have been for him to have yelled, "Shohei's here!"

At least when I got out to the garage, Shohei didn't mention what had happened.

"So what are we doing?" Shohei asked, looking up at the chicken-wire and two-by-four framework.

I showed him the diagram Shawna had made, then picked up one of the tissue squares. "Apply glue," I told him, "then insert into one of the chicken-wire holes, according to the design." I demonstrated by inserting the tissue as a flower shape into one of the hexagons.

"We have to do this for each one?" Shohei asked. "That'll take —"

"Less than three weeks," I said, which was all the time we had left.

We managed to get a lot done over the next couple hours, although all it really did was show us how much more we had to do.

Finally, we went into the house for lunch.

Hans-Peter was in there, with a bunch of little labeled ramekins filled with seasonings. He added the contents of one to some ground beef in a bowl.

"What're you doing?" Shohei asked.

"Testing out seasoning mixtures for my Wurstfest entry," Hans-Peter said.

"Not going well?" I asked. He gave me a sharp look, to see whether I'd been trying to be insulting.

"No," he said. "But I was about to have lunch, anyway. Hot dogs. Want some?" Hans-Peter washed his hands, then pulled a pot off the stove and used a pair of tongs to take out a couple hot dogs, which he put on a plate.

"Sure!" Shohei said. "Got any ketchup?"

Hans-Peter and I were both appalled, but for separate reasons.

"Do you know what's in hot dogs?" I demanded.

"Ketchup?" Hans-Peter asked. "Where are you from?"

Shohei looked blank for a moment. Then he shrugged. "Palo Alto, originally."

"Ketchup is for french fries," Hans-Peter said, sternly.

"What's wrong with ketchup?" Shohei asked as the doorbell rang.

"Nothing," Hans-Peter replied. "But while you're at it, would you like some maple syrup on it, too?"

I went to answer the door because the rest of the executive committee was due to arrive, and because I didn't want to listen to Hans-Peter's idea of culinary perfection.

When I opened the door, Patrick Jarndyce and Doris Witkowski were standing there. Even though I didn't like them much, we definitely needed more workers.

I let them in and headed back to the kitchen.

"Oh, great! Lunch!" Patrick said, grabbing a hot dog.

"Hey!" I said. "That's *not* tofu!"

"Oh, you're *serious* about that?" Patrick asked just before he stuffed the hot dog into his mouth. "I thought we were just sort of pretending to make a point." Oblivious to my rising anger, he looked down at what he was eating. "Hey, this is really good. Needs ketchup, though."

I was getting ready to denounce him — of course we were serious, and if he wasn't he shouldn't be in the group — when Hans-Peter cut in.

"We don't believe in ketchup," he said, in a completely even tone that still somehow managed to convey utter contempt.

Hans-Peter

Discuss an item representative of your cultural heritage.

It has recently come to my attention that a disturbingly large number of Chicagoans are losing touch with their cultural heritage. I am referring to the improper use of condiments on the Chicago-style hot dog.

The Chicago-style hot dog is a unique and otherworldly confection of pure beef, poppy-seed bun, and choice toppings. (There is no such thing as a vegan Chicago-style hot dog.)

The recipe is not complicated. There is, however, one supreme, cardinal, unalterable, all-important rule: *You may not — under any circumstances whatsoever — adulterate your hot dog with that condiment known as ketchup, catsup, or any variation thereof.* Puréed tomato sugar-water is for french fries.

The recipe:

100% all-beef hot dog: This, of course, is the most important ingredient. People have been known to come to blows over which is the most superior. Personally, I prefer the frankfurters that come only from Little Swabia's Delicatessen

76

Kowalski. (I think Vienna is the largest-selling
brand. If Vienna is not available where you are,
and you cannot make it up to Delicatessen Kowalski, try some of the kosher varieties.) Note: Certain brands of grocery store hot dogs that claim
to be "all beef" have the texture of peanut butter
and the flavor of wet sand. These are unaccept-
able. Remember that a hot dog is a sausage,
in the Old World sense of the word.

Poppy-seed bun: This is essentially a plain, out-
of-the-bag, eight-to-a-pack, hot dog bun that
has poppy seeds on it. If you can't find a poppy-
seed bun, a plain one will do. Just don't get exotic
and try for whole wheat or potato or low carb or
other unnatural things like that.

Yellow mustard: The bright yellow, mass-
produced kind. Nothing stone-ground, handmade
by Alsatian monks, or foreign-sounding.

Sweet pickle relish: This comes in a jar and
looks like it glows in the dark.

Kosher dill pickle: Sliced in the long direction,
not cross-wise.

(Fresh) Onion, chopped: Again, we're talking
the basic yellow kind. Nothing white or red or pre-
tentious like shallots.

(Fresh) Tomatoes, thinly sliced: Ordinary red.
The new yellow hybrids are just weird.

Celery salt: Very important!

"Sport" peppers: These come in a jar. They (I think) are pickled serranos and, in any case, are optional.

To prepare: Steam, boil, or grill the hot dog. You can briefly steam the bun, too (but it should not be soggy). Then, insert hot dog into bun. Apply mustard, onions, pickle relish, pickle slice, tomatoes, sport peppers, and celery salt. Eat.

Final note: Chili and sauerkraut may be noble comestibles and worthy subjects of song and poetry and other accolades, but only strange people and/or New Yorkers put them on their hot dogs. They have no place on a Chicago-style hot dog.

Chapter 6

It's Not Over . . .

Hans-Peter

I managed to get out of school for my Peshtigo community interview without too many problems, although I was going to have to make up a missed history quiz.

I was scheduled to meet with a Mrs. Dagmar Brandenburg. The bio flyer the admissions committee sent me said she sang opera ("in the big leagues," Opa noted); was married to a physics professor at the University of Chicago; and had sent all six of her children to Peshtigo, only one of whom was currently there, in my year.

The only thing Freddie had said about the family was, "They're sending you to Castle Brandenburg? That's scary."

Opa dropped me off at the Brandenburgs' mansion. It was this enormous post-Victorian bungaloid in

Ravenswood Manor on a corner lot, looked about three stories tall, and had a black wrought-iron fence surrounding it that came right up to the sidewalk.

I opened the gate and headed up the walkway to the stairs. Taking a breath, I climbed to the porch and rang the doorbell. The formal chimes sounded like something out of a horror movie. A dog barked. The door opened.

A guy about my age, wearing frameless glasses, was standing there, one hand on the knob, another on the collar of this enormous gray dog. A Weimaraner.

"Hi," he said. "I'm Elias. Come on in. Mom's going to be a couple minutes late. She told me to take you to the kitchen and give you something to drink."

"I'm Hans-Peter," I replied, then followed him and the dog inside.

As he led me past a flight of polished wood stairs, we heard a screeching, grinding noise that sounded a lot like what happens when Opa tries to shift gears on his VW before pressing down all the way on his clutch.

The dog made a rumbling sound.

"Beastmaster, heel," Elias said.

The dog quieted.

"What was that?" I asked Elias, who was a couple paces ahead.

He glanced back at me, then abruptly took a left turn. I followed him into a living room that had a fireplace, a harpsichord, a piano, and a couple of twenty-something guys who looked a lot like Elias.

At least the guy with the nondescript brownish hair and glasses sitting at the piano did. The other guy, the one sitting on the chair and holding a violin, looked more like a cadaver. Pale skin, black hair. The two were both peering at a stack of music sheets leaning against the piano's music holder. More sheets were arranged on every other spare surface. The brown-haired guy was making marks with a pencil.

Elias went over to take a closer look.

"Touch it and die," the black-haired guy said without looking up.

Elias turned to me. "This is Johann Ambrosius. He works for the government. He has no sense of humor and no life."

"Why don't you go take your little friend someplace that isn't here?" Johann Ambrosius asked, his voice like January off the lake.

"His name's Hans-Peter," Elias replied, "and he's here for his Peshtigo interview."

Johann Ambrosius looked at me. "Fool," he said, shaking his head before focusing his attention back to the music sheets.

"I'm Christoph," the other said, holding out his hand.

As I shook it, Elias told me, "Christoph has too much of a sense of humor."

Christoph smiled.

"This is where the problem is," Johann Ambrosius said, tapping the music sheet. "The oboes."

"Nice to meet you," Christoph told me, then turned to the music and asked his brother incredulously, "You want *more* oboes?"

"Fewer," Johann Ambrosius replied in that same icy tone.

"Don't worry about them," Elias said. "Do you want something to drink?" Without waiting for an answer, he added, "Let's go to the kitchen."

As we headed into a dining room, I asked, "What are they doing?"

"They're writing a concerto for my parents' anniversary," Elias replied. "It's a little Johann Sebastian Bach . . . and a little Stevie Ray Vaughn. It's avant-garde."

"Oh," I said. "That's nice." And intimidating. Everyone Peshtigoan seemed to be brilliantly eccentric. Or eccentrically brilliant. Or both.

We headed through a butler's pantry and into the kitchen. There was a marble island and a lot of stainless steel.

"Have a seat," Elias said, opening the fridge. He handed me a Coke, and we sat on bar stools at the island. The dog curled up on the floor beside him. "So, why do you want to go to Peshtigo?"

"I thought your Mom was doing the interview," I told him, with a grin. "Why do *you* go to Peshtigo?"

He did a double-take, and I kicked myself. Figuratively. Insulting the son of the interviewer was probably *not* the best way to go.

But Elias was game. "My great-great-great-grandfather sold all the land that became the Peshtigo School to the Foundation that started the place. Actually, he sold it all to them and separately to three other people at the same time. They were going to hang him, but they decided to hire him to teach Business Methods and Political Influence instead." He shrugged. "Basically, it's a family thing."

"Yeah," I said. "Me, too. My cousin Frederika goes there."

"Wait a second," Elias replied, freezing in place. "Not Freddie Murchison-Kowalski?"

"Yeah," I said, uncertainly.

"Huh," he answered, almost to himself. "Who'd have thought?"

"What do you mean?" I asked, for some reason preparing to be insulted on Freddie's behalf. She was still my cousin, after all.

He looked apologetic. "No one's ever met Freddie's family. So everyone just sort of says she's been raised by wolves."

"Oh, please," I replied. "Wolves eat meat."

We laughed, even though it really wasn't that funny.

"She's a little *different,*" I said, finally. I was almost ready to tell him about her plans for a homecoming float when we were interrupted.

"Most interesting people are," came a voice from behind. "Different, that is." I nearly jumped out of my skin, but it was Johann Ambrosius, not Mrs. Brandenburg. He was holding a cordless phone. "You," he pointed at Elias, "have a telephone call. It's Honoria."

Elias blushed, then jumped up and grabbed the phone. "I'll be right back," he said, and stepped onto the back porch. Johann Ambrosius went back to his concerto, leaving me alone with the giant dog and the stainless steel appliances.

A few minutes later, Elias returned and walked over to this wood-and-glass cabinet that had a tube leading from it to a window.

"Can you give me a hand with this?" Elias asked, bending over to take a look at the thing. He pulled it slowly away from the window, so the tube was stretched out.

"Sure," I said. "What is it?"

"It's an observation hive," Elias said. "For honeybees. My friend Honoria and I are trying to see whether —"

"Wait," I interrupted, suddenly nervous. And not just about the Peshtigo School. I edged away from the hive.

84

"Did you say *bees*? Real, live, actual bees that I'm severely allergic to?"

Who keeps bees in their kitchen?

Elias looked up. "Well, yes," he said, "but I assume they're only a problem if they actually sting you?"

"Of course it's the sting," I said, making sure I knew where the door was. "It's not like I eat the things."

"Then you're fine," Elias replied, his voice trailing off as he examined the hive. "They're sealed in here and . . . hmm . . . well, that's interesting." He paused, glancing at me. "Now don't be alarmed. *Bad* dog." He grabbed the animal by the collar, began to move slowly toward the kitchen island, and pulled open a drawer.

"What's wrong?" I asked, almost whispering. I did not want to swell up to the size of a large pumpkin and stop breathing.

"Beastmaster VII has been chewing the access tube again," Elias replied, in the same hushed tone. "I don't think it's really a problem, because the bees are fairly docile and the tube doesn't look completely chewed through, but just in case, take this, and then move slowly toward the door."

He handed me a small medical-looking box.

"Epinephrine auto-injector?" I read aloud.

"In case you get stung," Elias replied, "give yourself a shot."

"I'm going to die," I said. "On my school interview, I'm going to die . . ."

"Oh, I wouldn't worry," he said. "You have more of a chance of being killed by lightning than a bee sting."

I was about to ask him if he'd noticed there wasn't actually a thunderstorm in the kitchen, when some avant-garde screeching came from the music room. Beastmaster VII didn't like it any more than he had the first time. He bolted out of Elias's grip and directly toward the beehive. I stood in horror as the dog tore the plastic tube from the window and knocked over the cabinet with a crash.

"Run!" Elias yelled.

I was already running. I pushed open the swinging door and ran through the butler's pantry until I reached the entry hall. Glancing back, still clutching the epinephrine auto-injector, I considered whether to wait for my interview or leave and survive.

Barking and Elias's and his brothers' voices came from the kitchen.

After a brief hesitation, I decided to stay. I had not come this far in the application process to run away from a bunch of scary hive insects. Still, I made sure the front door was unlocked and the injector was at the ready. Then I sat down on a little red velvet entryway chair. It had a good strategic view through to the kitchen door and back of the house and the entry stairway.

Oddly enough, the Brandenburgs reminded me of Freddie, sort of extreme and chaotic at the same time. I wondered if Peshtigo made people like that or if they went to Peshtigo because they were like that.

Moments later, a tall, solid-looking woman with good posture and black hair appeared at the top of the stairs and gracefully walked down. I stood to shake her hand as the voices from the kitchen subsided.

"You must be Hans-Peter," she said. "I love your family's deli."

"Thanks," I replied. That, at least, was somewhat encouraging. A little surreal, though, because she was completely ignoring the thumping and occasional screams coming from the kitchen and because I was still very worried about the bees.

"Now, then," she said. "Please turn around."

I stared, not sure I wanted my back to the kitchen.

She made a twirling motion with her index finger.

I spun.

"Very good," she said. "Now hold out your hands."

I put the injector in my back pocket and held out my hands, palms up.

"Over," she said.

I flipped them over, noticing Elias had emerged from the kitchen and was standing behind his mother.

Sorry, he mouthed at me.

"Very nice," she said. "You'll do." She gave Elias a hard

look. "Make sure you clean up whatever you were doing in the kitchen before your father gets home." As he nodded, she turned around and headed back toward the stairs.

"That's it?" I whispered, glancing at Elias.

He made a face and held an index finger to his lips in the universal gesture of "be quiet."

Mrs. Brandenburg turned around. "Mr. Yamada," she said, "the fact that you have been able to sit down here with my children for forty-five minutes without running away gibbering suggests you should get along quite nicely at Peshtigo. And, you wash your hands." She bowed, not deeply. "Have a pleasant evening. Elias will see you out."

As his mother serenely swept up the stairs, Elias opened the door.

"Gibbering?" I asked.

He looked a little sheepish. "If you do get in to Peshtigo, ask me sometime about Thomas Edgar William Cochrane IV and my sister Anna's science project featuring Bo, the friendly rattlesnake."

Freddie

"Did you have to go through all this?" Hans-Peter demanded, later at the deli.

"All what?" I replied.

"Interviews and insane people and bees!"

He seemed freaked, but filled me on about his Brandenburg interview.

"The Brandenburgs are unique," I told him, "but not *that* unique. If you want to go to the Peshtigo School, get used to it."

Because Prospective Students Day, and hence the USCACA protest about Ms. Wilson and the electrical experiments, was fast approaching, I had asked Shawna and Eleanor to meet me at the deli to finalize our plans.

But I still had to work at the deli, so Shawna and Eleanor took notes while I dictated instructions and placard text. Meanwhile, I was also busy stocking the shelves with those items that would appeal most to those who were partaking of the festivities of Wurstfest Chicago.

"What is going on here?" Opa interrupted. "What part of this am I paying for?"

"I'm getting paid?" I asked. This was news to me.

"Not for gossiping with your friends," Opa replied.

"I wasn't gossiping," I told him. "I'm stocking the shelves and also trying to figure out our next school protest."

"*Ja*, well," Opa replied. "You, get back to work. You —" and he glared at Shawna and Eleanor "— go home and do your homework or whatever it is you should be doing."

"We were waiting for Freddie so we could help build the float," Eleanor said.

"Then go across the street to the *konditerei*, have some coffee, and wait for her there," Opa replied. "She will be off at five o'clock."

As Eleanor and Shawna trudged off, Opa told me he was going down to see the Do Your Wurst people about something, and that the health inspector was coming, but that Hans-Peter and Mrs. Fraunhofer knew what to do.

The health inspector — whose name was Bernard Holtzman — showed up at four-thirty. Mrs. Fraunhofer was taking another of her coffee breaks, so Hans-Peter was manning the cash register. Ernst took Holtzman around the butcher area in the back, where all the potential health code violations would be. Except, oh right, even the Centers for Disease Control weren't as clean as Opa's deli.

So, after a while, Holtzman strolled back up front, tore a sheet off his clipboard, and handed it to Hans-Peter. "Tell Willi I'll see him next time."

As Holtzman headed out the front door, Hans-Peter called after him. "Wait, you dropped this." He held out a brown envelope that had been sitting on the counter.

Holtzman gave a grin, then said, "Oh, thank you."

"No, he didn't forget it," I blurted. "The envelope was sitting there before he arrived."

Hans-Peter gave me a look. "No, it wasn't."

"Yes, it was," I insisted.

"Is there a problem?" Holtzman asked, glancing from Hans-Peter to me.

"No," Hans-Peter said firmly.

Holtzman took the envelope, then left.

"What did you think you were doing?" Hans-Peter demanded.

"What was in the envelope?" I replied. "He didn't leave it."

"Of course he didn't leave it," Hans-Peter said. "It's just something you say when you're making the drop."

"What?"

He shook his head impatiently. "Making the drop. Giving him a little something for the missus. Or —"

"Do you mean to say," I interrupted, discretely lowering my voice despite my outrage, "that you're *bribing* the health inspector?"

"*Shh,*" Hans-Peter said, glancing around. "We don't like to call it that."

"But that's what it is, right?" I was appalled. I'd thought that sort of thing had gone out sometime back in the olden days. Like 1975.

"It's more like . . ." Hans-Peter paused. "A gratuity."

"But . . . but . . . why? The place is totally clean!"

"Well, yes," Hans-Peter said, "but that doesn't mean he can't still shut us down."

"That's so —" I began, then saw Opa enter through the front. "Opa!"

He walked over to Hans-Peter and me.

"Are you *bribing* the health inspector?" I asked, making sure the other customers couldn't hear me.

Opa whacked Hans-Peter on the head with his Cubs cap. "What have you been telling your cousin?"

"What was in the envelope?" I demanded.

"Five hundred dollars," Opa said. "Cash money."

"Then it was a bribe!"

"It was not a bribe," Opa said. At this point, Hans-Peter was starting to lose it. "Bernard is also city representative on the Little Swabia Chamber of Commerce," Opa explained. "The money was for the Wurstfest entertainment. The deli is a sponsor."

By now, Hans-Peter could barely stand, he was laughing so hard. "The look on your face," he gasped.

"So," I said, ignoring Hans-Peter and just to make sure, "you *aren't* bribing the health inspector?"

Opa shook his head. "It has been many years since we have had to bribe the health inspector."

"Honest?"

"Honest," Opa said. "Now we just give freebies to the precinct captain."

At this point, I was positive Opa was joking.

"It is almost five," Opa said. "Why don't you find your friends from across the street and go work on your float?"

I did.

Hans-Peter

By the time Opa and I got home after an evening of working on Wurstfest preparations, Freddie's friends had left and the float was shaping up into something resembling her plan. The problems began when Opa and I went into the dining room and the living room. The furniture was where it was supposed to be, but the floors showed bare hardwood.

Freddie was sitting in one of the armchairs, curled up with a book.

"Frederika," Opa said, remarkably calmly, "where are the rugs?"

"I rolled them up and put them in the basement."

"Why would you do this?" Opa asked.

"Because I can't be true to my vegan principles and walk on wool any more," Freddie said, as if it were plainly obvious.

"I see," Opa said in a considering tone. "And the fact that it was your chore to vacuum the rugs had nothing to do with this?"

"No," Freddie said with a sniff.

"Well," Opa said, "that is something." Then he raised his voice. "Bring them back! Now! Go!"

Freddie stared.

"Why are you still sitting there! *Schnell!*"

"But —" Freddie began as she got up.

"I do not want to hear it!" Then Opa looked at me. "You! Help her! Both of you! Move! Get the furniture out of the way and bring the rugs back."

"I didn't do anything," I protested.

"I did not ask for feedback," Opa said. "Go!"

Opa started back to the kitchen while Freddie and I began to move the furniture. Then we went down to the basement to bring the rugs upstairs. We had just hauled the living room rug up the stairs when Opa stopped us.

"Wait," he said. "I have decided. Before the rugs go back, you will clean them first. The old-fashioned way."

"What do you mean?" Freddie asked.

"I mean you will take them outside and drape them over the clothesline and beat them with a stick until they are clean."

"What?" we exclaimed simultaneously.

"Now!"

So Freddie and I hauled the rug outside to the clothesline. Opa handed us two softball bats and we got to work.

"Are you happy now?" I asked Freddie as dust and cat hair rose off the rug.

"I didn't do anything wrong," she said, clenching her jaw as she hit away.

"If this is your idea of getting back at me for the honey and bouillon cubes," I muttered, "it didn't work out too well."

Freddie ground her teeth. "When I really get back at you, you'll know it."

Chapter 7

Life, Death, and Eden

Hans-Peter

The Peshtigo School admissions tour was, of course, on a school day, which didn't bother me at all. The school tour started with an auditorium pep talk and historical video. I met Shohei, who was supposed to be my tour guide, afterward, outside. (We were supposed to have met beforehand, inside.)

"All set?" Shohei asked. "First up's the Advanced Methods in History of Science class with Ms. Wilson."

He led me down the hallway until a rather large and apparently excitable faculty member jumped out of a classroom and yelled, "Shohei! What did you do with the alpenhorn?"

Through the open door, I could hear a classroom of people yodeling in concert.

Shohei winced. "Music theory," he explained. "Why

don't you go down to Ms. Wilson's class, Room two-twenty-one, and I'll meet you there?"

Shohei headed into the classroom with the music teacher while I tried to figure out the map. The Peshtigo School had a grade school division and a high school division, which were largely in separate buildings but which shared some faculty and facilities.

The grade school, which we were going to see in the morning, was built around this large atrium courtyard that was filled with tropical plants. In the afternoon, we'd cross the bridge and see the high school. Overall, the place was a lot newer, larger, and had more of the modern bells and whistles than my current school, which was built during the Great Depression.

I made my way up to Room 221, and discovered, unpleasantly, that Freddie, Shawna, and Eleanor were already at the door, carrying placards and apparently ready to pounce. Eleanor and Shawna were wearing black, like Freddie, and holding up signs that said STOP THE KILLING! and END THE CARNAGE!

"What are you doing?" I demanded.

"Why are *you* here?" Freddie replied.

"School tour," I said, hand on the door. I glanced at my watch, then paused. "Could you give me at least five minutes before you barge in and do whatever you're planning?"

To my surprise, she nodded. "No promises, though."

"Thank you," I said, figuring it was the best I could do, then entered.

The teacher was wearing a lab coat, standing in front of a lab table. The first thing I noticed, though, was the four frog legs hanging from a metal frame.

"Notice the 'dancing,'" the teacher said as she prodded them with a scalpel that was wired to a battery. One by one, the legs spasmed, twitched, and kicked. "Luigi Galvani called this phenomenon 'animal electricity,' and he thought —"

Possibly I was a little on edge. Possibly I was worried about being admitted to the Peshtigo School. Possibly it was because Freddie was there, with her placards and protest. Possibly it was because at least one of the legs had the *same* scar that Euclid had. Otherwise, I'm almost positive, I wouldn't have yelled, "Where did you get those frogs?"

"Who are you?" the teacher asked.

At this moment, fortunately or unfortunately, Freddie and her gang of two stormed into the room, waving their placards.

"What do you think you're doing?" Freddie asked, almost shouting. "What did you do to those frogs? Where's the rest of them?"

"Where did you get them?" I repeated.

The teacher looked baffled. "They're from the Midwest Seafood House," she said "Who are you, again?"

"I'm with them," I said, pointing at Freddie. I was definitely not going to give my real name. At least, though, I knew she hadn't killed Euclid and Pythagoras.

Unfortunately, the next words out of Freddie's mouth were, "What's next? Dissecting puppies?"

"Freddie," the teacher said, "take your entourage and go bother Mr. Eden."

Freddie didn't wait. She turned her back and marched out the door, Shawna and Eleanor behind her. A second later, I followed.

"Aren't you supposed to have more people here?" I asked when we got outside.

Freddie gave me a look. It was a look that said "Stop your blathering, I have more important things to do." It was spooky. "Come with me," she said.

Shawna, Eleanor, and I followed.

She led us on to a gym that had a picture of a penguin with a sword on the wall. A bunch of tables with signs for a bunch of student clubs had been set up under the penguin. Freddie walked up to the table displaying the banner for the Union of Students Concerned About Cruelty to Animals.

"What is going on?" she demanded of Patrick and Doris. "What happened with the protest? Where is everyone?"

"Hi," Patrick said, ignoring Freddie and standing to shake my hand. "I'm Patrick Jarndyce —"

"You already know him," spooky Freddie said. "You stole his lunch the other day. Now, answer my question."

Her tone caught Patrick's attention. He glanced over, then spoke. "We found out this morning we have the opportunity to set up a work-study volunteering at the Humane Society. We held an emergency meeting of the executive committee this morning and decided we didn't want to jeopardize the chance by making a futile protest. Sorry we weren't able to let you know in time."

I couldn't tell whether the last comment was directed at Freddie, Eleanor, or Shawna.

"It's a good thing I'm a vegan and don't believe in harming even the most vicious, unappealing creatures," Freddie said, then walked off.

Shawna, Eleanor, and I followed. Again.

"Wait," I asked. "Where are Euclid and Pythagoras?"

Freddie hesitated, then glanced at Eleanor.

"They're not waiting to be dissected somewhere, are they?" I didn't think this was likely, but you never knew.

"No, they're not," Freddie said, finally. "They're in the fountain in the garden."

At that moment, Shohei reappeared. "Where did you go? You were supposed to be in Ms. Wilson's class." Before waiting for an answer, he forged ahead. "Come on, you're scheduled for the grand tour."

I followed, leaving Freddie and her friends behind.

"This place is so weird," I muttered as he led me through the hall toward the center of the school. A group was already gathered in front of a wrought-iron gate. A bald, lanky man wearing a sweater vest stood with his hand on the latch. He seemed to be in a bad mood.

"Mr. Eden," Shohei whispered.

"You will not take food or drink into the Garden," Mr. Eden said. "You will not touch anything. You will not enter with a musical instrument or electronic device of any kind, genus, form, or species whatsoever. You will not sing, hum, whistle, chant, gargle, or speak above a whisper. If you do so, you will be forever banished from the Peshtigo School. Is that clear?"

When he heard the mutterings of assent, he opened the gate.

"Oh," he said, turning around. "One final thing: Do not disturb the cats."

Softly, over the noise of a fountain, we heard some kind of elevator music.

"As you can see," Mr. Eden said from the front of the group, "we have an exceptional collection of hurricane and cabbage palms . . ."

Somehow, Shohei and I had gotten to the back of the group. I grabbed him by the arm. "I want to look at that fountain," I said.

"Why?"

I explained briefly about Freddie and the frogs. And Ms. Wilson and the frogs. And that mine were supposed to be in the fountain.

As we edged over, Shohei muttered, "You really need to meet my friend Honoria."

As we reached the fountain, I read the plaque that called it the "Fountain of the Grand Army of the Republic." It looked like Buckingham Fountain, only smaller, with a large main basin and a couple of smaller basins rising from the center. At the top was a small geyser. Three dolphins spewed water from the lower basin up to the top, which then waterfalled back down. The main basin was filled with lily pads and small fish that kept darting in and out of the shadows.

I was facing the fountain, trying to figure out where I'd hide if I were a bullfrog, when I heard a cat yowl, and then Shohei yelled and knocked into me at the same time. Already kind of off balance, I toppled into the fountain, banging my forehead on something as I plunged into the water. I came up coughing, on my hands and knees, as I felt claws dig into my back when what I guessed was the cat jumped off.

"What did you do?" I sputtered to Shohei between coughs.

"Um, you're bleeding," he said.

I stood, then leaned back against the upper basin and put my hand to my forehead where the pain was coming from. It came off with a bit of water and more blood.

An alarm had sounded.

As I tried to wade my way past some crumpled lily pads, Mr. Eden appeared.

"What are you doing? Who told you you could go in there?" he asked, rapid fire. "Who set off the alarm? Do you *realize* what this is doing to the plants? Get out of there this instant, before the lawyers arrive!"

"Stay right where you are!" came another voice behind Mr. Eden. "No one move!"

The new arrival was this guy with a briefcase, wearing a lapel-mike walkie-talkie, leading two guys with clipboards and one woman with a camera. Behind them came an older guy wearing a stethoscope and carrying a black bag.

"Stay right there," Briefcase Guy said. "We need to make sure we don't taint the scene. You —" he pointed at the woman with the camera "— start taking pictures."

The guys with the clipboards fanned out and began asking the other students questions.

"Do *not* step on the plants!" Mr. Eden said, following after.

"Hi, I'm Dr. Bob," the guy with the stethoscope said. "That's quite a cut you've got. Let me take a look at that. Can you see me okay? Any blurry vision? Ringing in your ears?"

"Wait!" Briefcase Guy screamed, shoving Shohei out of the way. "Do we have authorization? We need parental consent to treat him! Don't touch him! You! In the fountain! You're one of the applicants, right? What's your name?"

I told him, then he called into his lapel mike. "Lucy, I need a check on medical authorization for a Hans-Peter Yamada! Yes! Immediately!"

Dr. Bob handed me a gauze pad. "Hold this to your forehead." He gestured at Briefcase Guy. "That's Jim Jarndyce. Esquire. He's one of our louder parent volunteer lawyers. Ignore him."

Thirty seconds later, Jarndyce got the vacant look of someone listening to an earpiece. "Doc, you're okay to go," he barked. "Don't kill him."

"I rarely do," Dr. Bob said, then took at look at my forehead. "That doesn't look too bad. Shouldn't need stitches."

"So, tell me, what happened?" Jarndyce asked, oozing concern, while Dr. Bob poured some liquid on a gauze pad.

"I don't know," I said. Behind him, Shohei was either trying to give me signals of some kind or had developed a facial tic. "There was this yowl . . . a cat, I think . . . and who are you again?"

Jarndyce made some notes while Dr. Bob held out the gauze. "This may sting a little. Just some antiseptic to clean that up."

It stung, but not bad. Then he pressed a bandage in place. "Good as new," he said. "Just one thing —"

"What?" Jarndyce barked. "Good as new? Did you read the memo? What about a concussion? Look, he's shivering! And he's babbling about cats! We have no cats!"

"He's standing in a fountain," Dr. Bob said. "He's probably cold."

"Yeah, can I get out now?" I asked.

"Yes," Dr. Bob mouthed at me.

"What about the cats?" Jarndyce demanded.

"We have cats," Mr. Eden said, "because we have mice. Now, take your people and get out of my garden."

"Why do we have mice?" Jarndyce demanded.

"If you do start noticing anything over the next few days, call your family doctor," Dr. Bob said, helping me out of the fountain and handing me a brochure titled *How to Recognize Traumatic Brain Injury and What to Do About It.*

"He's going to sue us!" I heard Jarndyce muttering to the photographer on their way out. "I've seen it before. I just know he's going to sue us. He'll want us to pay for plastic surgery and emotional distress because we messed up his career as a face model. . . ."

"You wouldn't happen to have a towel, would you?" I asked Dr. Bob.

"Shohei, get him some gym clothes from the school store," Dr. Bob said. "Meet us back at the clinic."

As Shohei was heading off, he ran into some brown-haired girl.

"Oh, hi, Honoria," Shohei said. He gestured back at me. "That's Hans-Peter, Freddie's cousin. Gotta go."

"I understand you fell into the fountain," Honoria said to me.

"Yeah," I replied, wondering if the entire place was under twenty-four-hour video surveillance, although possibly the fact that I was dripping wet gave a clue.

"Before you leave," she said, "Jim Jarndyce will try to get you to sign a release. Do not do so until your family lawyer has a chance to look at it."

"What?"

"Don't sign anything," she repeated. Then she looked hard at me and Dr. Bob. "And this conversation never took place." With that, she turned and marched off.

I glanced at Dr. Bob.

"What conversation?" he asked, as we exited the garden.

Freddie

I led Eleanor and Shawna to one of the library conference rooms. Work-study at the Humane Society. Right. Patrick had ditched our protest on purpose.

This was about power.

"He's lying," Shawna said.

I bit back the urge to say "Of course he's lying," because Shawna was new and therefore had probably been giving Patrick the benefit of the doubt until now.

"We have to do something about him," Eleanor said.

"I know," I replied. "Suggestions?" The problem was that all Peshtigo School student organizations were open to anyone.

Eleanor pulled out her copy of the Uniform Peshtigo School Student Organization Bylaws. "According to this," she said, "there are only two ways to get rid of someone. One, if he is no longer enrolled. Two, if he voluntarily quits."

After a moment, Shawna asked, "how do we get him expelled?"

I laughed. "I like the way you think."

Eleanor looked worried. "You're not serious, right?"

Sometimes Eleanor could be too literal.

"No," I said. "We just need to make him want to quit." I got up to look out the window. "Preferably, immediately after the homecoming parade."

"Why after?" Eleanor asked.

"Because," I said as we headed out, "we still need his help to finish building the float."

Chapter 8

Three Point One Four . . .

Freddie

After weeks of work, we finally finished — not quite at the last minute.

"We're done!" Shohei yelled around midnight as he placed the last of approximately a quarter million squares of blue and white tissue paper (the foamy sea) onto our float.

As Shohei and Marcus high-fived, Opa and Hans-Peter walked into the garage. I was sort of expecting Opa but surprised to see Hans-Peter, since the Peshtigo School application exam was also tomorrow. He needed a good night's sleep and all that.

"Ah, you're done! Very good," Opa said. "Now we can put the float on the trailer and you can all leave my house."

"But we're not finished," Doris protested, holding up

the can of clear-coat finish she and Patrick had brought that morning. It was their big contribution to our supplies inventory, although Patrick had said he'd stolen it from his artist sister. I'd already told them "no" once.

"My father always says, anything worth doing is worth doing right," Patrick said.

"You are done," Opa told them, staring until they nodded in agreement.

No one else dared say anything.

Quickly we got everyone organized around the float and heaved it on top of the trailer. Then Marcus crawled underneath, tightened a few bolts, and it was secure.

Hans-Peter

Friday morning, Opa dropped me off at the corner before he went to work. The Peshtigo admissions test was supposed to last all day long.

I got to the classroom ten minutes before it was scheduled to start. The proctor was seated behind a gray metal desk at the front of the room. More than half of the seats were already occupied by prospective students. A stack of bubble sheets, a notepad, and several sharpened yellow pencils had been placed on each of the desks. A note on the green chalkboard told those entering to be seated according to the name tags on the desks. I found mine and unpacked my mechanical pencils and drafting eraser. There wasn't a lot of conversation. Only one out of the seven of us would be getting in.

At precisely eight o'clock, a bell rang, and the proctor stood up. "Good morning," he said. "It is now time for your Peshtigo admissions exam."

A couple of voices said "good morning" in return. A girl next to me cleared her throat. I tightened my grip on my pencil.

"I'm Mr. Bellini," he went on. "We have something of a change in plan, I'm afraid." He smiled. "Due to a minor glitch, you won't be taking the standard exam this morning."

The girl across the aisle from me sighed, and a tall guy with an English accent wanted to know why we were there at all, then.

Mr. Bellini held up his hand. "We do have something else in mind for this phase of admissions. We were able to get in touch with a distinguished alumnus who put together a problem for us."

The chattering subsided.

"Listen very carefully," he said. "In a moment, I will write something on the board. You will copy it down, and you will be silent while you do so. You will then leave, still without talking. You have one day." He smiled. "One *sidereal* day — to prepare a response. Assume no eccentricities. You must obey the Peshtigo School honor code. You may not discuss this with anyone or use the Internet. You must submit your response to the Peshtigo School's drop box. We will not accept late answers. Period."

He grabbed a piece of chalk, then wrote on the chalkboard:

MAY I HAVE A DIGIT, PERCHANCE?
PI.
MAKETH THINE OWN, GOING ONWARDLY.
SEQUENCED.

It looked like gibberish.

"Easy as pi," the guy next to me said, exuding confidence.

"What did you say?" Mr. Bellini demanded, walking over to stand in front of him.

"Easy as pi?" the guy said, swallowing hard.

"Mr. Zaret," Mr. Bellini said, reading the guy's name tag. "You are dismissed. Your application will be updated to reflect its incompleteness."

"What?" Zaret looked shocked.

"You are in violation of the honor code and application procedures," Mr. Bellini said. "The Peshtigo School does not tolerate people of low character."

Suddenly, you could hear the hum of traffic outside.

Mr. Bellini glanced around and snapped, "The rest of you have work to do."

I wrote down the problem, then checked the clock: 8:10 AM. We had twenty-three hours and fifty minutes to hand in our answers.

I exited. In silence.

Freddie

Eleanor's sixteen-year-old brother, Franklin Delano (Yes, their real names. Yes, I think their parents were cruel), had volunteered to drive our float to school for the pre-homecoming lineup and then tomorrow for the actual parade. He and Eleanor arrived with the family pickup just after Hans-Peter headed out for his test.

Anyway, I opened the garage door so Del could back up to the hitch. When we got the trailer hooked up without a problem, we connected the compressor and snaked the control box into the pickup cab. This, too, went off without a hitch. So to speak.

With the three of us in the cab and Eleanor sitting next to her brother, we figured we should test the float under live conditions. Del put the truck in gear, then began to pull the float out of the garage.

When the float was clear of the garage door, Eleanor

hit the "on" switch. The compressor made a chugging noise, and the blowfish began to inflate, as it had done the night before.

"Beware! Beware the seas! Or none will survive!" spoke the loudspeakers. A nice last-minute touch, I have to say.

When the blowfish expanded to where it should have stopped inflating, though, instead of the failsafe switch kicking in, and deflating, there was a loud whine and a shudder, and it continued to grow. Gigantic. Wheezing. Threatening.

"Beware! Beware the seas! Or none will survive!"

I pressed the off switch on the control box.

The whine grew louder and more high-pitched.

"What's that?" Del asked, looking back through his rearview mirror.

"Turn it off!" Eleanor yelled.

"Trying," I muttered, jabbing at the useless button. "Nothing's happening!"

Then I heard a clunk as Del's truck lurched to a stop. "What did you do?" he demanded, looking back at the blowfish float, which was still inflating.

Bigger and bigger.

"Turn off your truck!" I said, trying to be calm and definitely not yelling.

"It went off by itself," Del said. "Which, by the way, isn't supposed to happen!"

"No kidding," Eleanor muttered.

"Duck!" Del yelled, then pushed us down on the seat next to him, below the cab's rear window, as the whine became a hiss.

The blowfish kept inflating and the loudspeakers kept going *"Beware! Beware the . . ."* until, finally, *BANG!* Something crashed into the back window. The glass cracked, but didn't shatter. We stayed down, though, until the loudspeakers quieted and the hiss stopped.

"Is everyone okay?" I asked.

"Yeah," Del said while Eleanor nodded shakily.

I released my seat belt and jumped out of the truck.

The blowfish had exploded. Pieces of it were scattered a good way back in the alley and also hanging from nearby trees. A large chunk of the fish head and the left eye were resting on top of Mr. Periwinkle's garage. His dogs were barking and tearing at a piece of the tail that had fallen into their backyard.

"I guess that's it," Eleanor said from the other side of the truck. "So much for the parade."

"I guess," I said.

But something in me wasn't ready to give up. The float looked bad, true, but the sharks were still mostly okay. They must have been shielded from the main blast.

"There's no way we can rebuild the blowfish in time," Eleanor said.

True. But I remembered all the hours and late nights

we had spent stuffing tissue into chicken wire. I would not surrender.

"Come on," I said, leading Del and Eleanor into the basement and Opa's workshop. I pulled out Opa's reciprocating saw. "Ever use one of these?" I asked Del, handing it to him.

"Sure," he said. "Why?"

Stepping outside the workshop, I turned on the lights to the rest of the basement. "That," I said, pointing at Rex, "is our new float. But we need to get it through the door." Hans-Peter wouldn't mind, I decided. Too much, anyway. Besides, he owed me for the honey, shampoo, and bouillon cubes, not to mention the health inspector. And this was for a good cause.

"It's perfect!" Eleanor exclaimed. "Why is it here?"

"Don't ask," I said. "Get on the phone and call everyone. We've still got work to do."

Hans-Peter

That guy, Zaret, getting punted from Peshtigo admissions for an honor code violation was freaking me out. Plus, already baffled by the exam problem, I didn't want to have to deal with Freddie, too. I knew she and her committee would be putting the finishing touches on their float, so I decided to work at the Sulzer Library for a few hours before going home.

A good idea in principle, but I didn't actually get anywhere.

Later, when I got home, Freddie was doing homework in the living room.

"You're back early," she observed. "Did you leave in the middle of it?"

"No," I said. "And thanks for the vote of confidence."

She made an impatient gesture. "What happened?"

"They gave us a single question, riddle, problem, whatever, and we have only twenty-four hours!" I looked at the mantle clock, *"Eighteen* hours, now, to solve it."

I'd already wasted six.

"Can I see?" she asked as we headed into the kitchen.

"No," I told her. "The honor code . . ."

"Doesn't say anything about showing copies of the test to other people . . ."

"Yes, it does," I replied. "You're not allowed to see it, comment on it, help out with it, or anything other than let me flounder around feeling dumb as a stone. Because that's the way they do things at Peshtigo."

"Fine," she said. "Suit yourself."

"I will," I told her, grabbing a Coke from the fridge. "And now I'm going downstairs to try to type something up. Bye."

"Wait a minute," she said, suddenly blocking the door.

"What's going on?" I asked.

"Nothing," she said. "Umm. It's just damp and cold down there and —"

"You're a terrible liar," I told her. "What did you do?"

She opened the door and led the way down the stairs. At the bottom, she flipped on the light, "Look at all this space you have down here now!"

It felt like my eyes were bugging out.

Where Rex had lain, sort of resting on its side for the past couple years, now there was nothing there except a bare spot on the concrete. "You . . . you . . . keep taking my stuff."

"Well," Freddie said in a rush, "we had an accident with the blowfish, so I figured, you know, two birds . . ."

I don't have time for this, I thought. I really do *not* have time for this. I managed to control my outrage. "Tomorrow," I told her, in a nice, even tone of voice, "it comes back. Right there, the same as it was before!" Without waiting for an answer, I turned to go back upstairs. Then something occurred to me. "Wait a minute," I said. "How did you get it out the door?"

"Two pieces," Freddie replied. "Reciprocating saw."

"You cut it in half?" I whispered.

"It was the only way —"

"Are you *kidding*?" I asked, furious, then charged on without waiting for a reply. "Do you even *think* about things before you do them? Do you care about other people at all?" As she opened her mouth to argue, I interrupted. "Just bring it back! Bring it back! For once in your life, fix something! I have to go do my test."

Eleven o'clock at night. I'd been given twenty-four hours to come up with an answer, and thanks to Freddie, I'd already wasted a bunch of them. Well, not wasted, but I hadn't gotten anywhere on a solution. I was at my desk in my bedroom, the problem written down in front of me.

I was deeply worried I didn't know nearly as much as everyone else taking the test. Easy as pi. Easy as the ratio of a circle's diameter to its circumference. Ha.

Pi. I decided to start from the beginning.

May I have a digit perchance? Essentially, it meant, please may I have a digit? Then, pi. Pi wasn't a digit, but it had digits. An infinite number of them. People had been trying to come up with more and more digits since they invented numbers. More, since computers came on the scene.

Maketh thine own. Obviously, make your own. But, make your own what?

Going onwardly. Sequenced. Continue in sequence. Or put it in sequence? But the sequence had to be pi, in a way that I had madeth mine own. If "madeth" was a word.

I didn't know how to calculate pi.

I wrote it down, right above the problem: 3.141592653589 . . .

It didn't help.

I knew you could get to pi indirectly by some converging series and making all kinds of huge calculations, but that didn't help, either.

I started drawing circles and inscribing polygons inside them. Then I started drawing polygons and inscribing circles inside them. Then I decided that method wasn't going to get me anywhere near a decent, accurate number of digits for pi, especially by eight the next morning.

So I sat there, staring. I don't know how long. Hours.

The words.

The numbers.

The words and the numbers.

Finally, I got up to grab another Coke and a bagel from the fridge. Opa's crossword puzzle was sitting on the kitchen table. As I popped the top of the can, I thought, "What's a three-point-one-four-letter word for 'I feel like an idiot'?"

And then I had it. The solution. I ran back into my room and saw what I'd written. What the Peshtigo test-writing fiend had written. And what would happen when the words and the numbers were lined up:

3.   1   4   1   5   9   2   6   5
MAY I HAVE A DIGIT PERCHANCE? PI. MAKETH THINE
  3   5   8   9 . . .
OWN, GOING ONWARDLY. SEQUENCED.

I wasn't supposed to calculate the digits of pi. In fact, how could I, unless I was some kind of math genius? I paused for a moment, but figured that probably no one applying would be able to do that, and I didn't have time anyway. No, focus. I looked at my alarm clock. It was four in the morning.

What they wanted was a mnemonic. To symbolize the digits of pi.

Each word in the problem had the same number of letters as the corresponding digit of pi. *May.* A three-letter word. *I.* A one-letter word. *Have.* A four-letter word. And so on. That was the answer — for me to come up with my own mnemonic. Beyond the one in the problem itself.

I'd figured it out.

Or at least figured out what I was supposed to figure out.

I ran downstairs to type it up.

While the computer booted, I glanced at the vacant space in the basement where Rex used to be. I was going to have to do something about Freddie. But later.

One problem at a time.

I looked at the clock in the corner of the computer screen: 4:12 AM. I didn't know if I could make it in time. I'd try, though. Boy, would I try.

By the time Opa and Freddie got up at six, I still had nothing coherent and I'd had so much caffeine my teeth were vibrating.

They left.

Some time later, I had this:

  3 1 4 1 5   9   2   6   5
How I want a solid chocolate or nougat bunny;
  3   5   8   9
and maybe brightly decorated.
   7   9 3 2 3   8
Sausage sometimes can be too tempting.
 4 6 2 6   4
Diet brings to sorrow many.
 3 3   8 3 2 7   9
But the problems for me perhaps resulting
 5   0   2 8
would [relatively] be terrible.
   8   4 1 9   7
Veganism must I dutifully embrace.

Okay, it was really bad, but it was free verse, so who could tell?

I fudged on the zero digit by giving the word "relatively" ten letters, but I figured that would be kind of all right. I also figured I wouldn't have time to take the El all the way down to Peshtigo, so I called Opa while I printed out my answer. He told me he'd be able to drive me to the school if I could get myself to the deli. If my luck held, I would just be able to make the deadline.

I slipped my solution in an envelope, grabbed my coat and ran out the door. I heard a train in the distance. I told myself it was going the wrong way, but ran faster anyway. I got to the station, fed my card into the machine, and made it onto the platform.

Looking down the track, I could see the light of a train just past Kedzie. I jumped aboard as soon as the doors opened and stared at my watch the entire time I was on the train, a whole five minutes.

When the train pulled in, two stops down, I dashed out and down the stairs, dodging the one or two people up that early on a Saturday. When I got to the deli, Opa was at the slicing machine, and Freddie was up front with Mrs. Fraunhofer sweeping up.

"Are you ready?" I asked Opa.

He looked over. "Ernst called in sick. We've got to finish up here for the Schutzes' wedding. They are coming by this morning. *Schlachtplatte* and *wurstplatte*. The wurst is yet to come."

I ignored the terrible pun. "I've got thirty-five minutes to get this downtown!" I exclaimed, or maybe shouted. I felt like an insane person. I hadn't showered, and my teeth felt furry.

Opa hesitated. Then he made a decision. "You finish up here. The cold cuts list is on the table over there. I'll get to the sausage order." He wiped his hands on his apron. "But do not tell your mother."

I nodded.

Mom did not want me using the slicing, cutting, or chopping machines at the deli, even though I'd done it before under Opa's supervision.

I took off my jacket, put on an apron, and looked at the list. Opa had stopped in the middle of a pound of smoked turkey, sliced thin. The smoked turkey was almost gone; only a small chunk was left. I grabbed it, turned on the machine, and began to slice.

I'm not sure what happened next. Suddenly, the turkey was gone, and so was the plastic guard, and my hand was in the way. I felt an icy sensation and then saw blood everywhere. It took me a minute to realize it was mine. My *blood*.

Pulling my hand back, I yelled, "Opa!"

I held my hand to my chest, feeling a lot of pain and trying to stop the flow of blood.

Opa rushed in, sized up the situation. He grabbed

a couple of clean towels and wrapped my hand. "Mrs. Fraunhofer!" he roared. "You're in charge! I'll be back! Family emergency! Ravenswood Hospital!" He rushed me out the back door to his Volkswagen.

Woozy. I felt woozy. Nothing seemed quite real.

Suddenly, a voice called out. "Wait, Hans-Peter, did you submit your answer?"

Freddie.

I opened my eyes. Freddie, looking pale, was right there, but she was waving around like I was seeing her through gasoline vapor. "If you didn't, I can take it down there. By eight, right?"

"Coat pocket," I whispered. Then I felt Opa put the VW in gear, and that was the last thing I remembered.

Freddie

I grabbed the envelope from Hans-Peter's jacket pocket and ran over to the El station.

I looked at my watch. No time to spare.

Fortunately, the train arrived just as I got to the platform. As the doors closed, I tried to figure out the best way to get down to the Peshtigo School. The Ravenswood Brown line didn't end up anywhere near the right place. I could transfer to the subway at Belmont, but then I'd have to wait for another train. Or, I could try to get a cab there and head straight down Lake Shore Drive and hope traffic was moving.

I hopped off the train at Belmont, spotted a cab, and took it. And I didn't feel any guilt about jumping in ahead of the lady with the mink coat.

I had the cabbie let me off at the drop box — basically a large mail slot in the office wall of the Peshtigo School. As I dropped in Hans-Peter's answer, his admissions on the line, I checked my watch. Four minutes past eight o'clock.

Too late!

I leaned against the wall, deflated. Hans-Peter was not going to get in, but . . . I'd done the best I could. All I could do now was go on over to the stadium for the parade setup. As for Hans-Peter, he'd get over it, his hand would heal, and everything would be fine.

For some reason, I paused. Maybe it was because I'd stolen his stupid dinosaur and taken his frogs. But something was wrong and I needed to think.

The Peshtigo School office was the only area of the school open to the public and, for that reason, was not exactly a high-tech operation (I think the administration didn't want to frighten casual visitors).

Since there was a drop box, there had to be someone to empty it, and whoever was responsible wouldn't necessarily do that exactly at eight. In fact, the box should have been locked precisely then. I shouldn't have been able to drop off Hans-Peter's test answer. Which meant, it must have gotten in unofficially on time.

Again, I was ready to head off. But I had to check. I had to be sure.

I ran to the door next to the main office and began pounding.

After too long a time, it opened.

A middle-aged woman I didn't recognize frowned at me. "What is it?"

"Hi," I said, trying to fake being out of breath. "I'm a student here and I'm here for the homecoming parade and could you let me in a second, please? I need to pee." I tried hard to look like someone who needed to pee. I figured only a truly cruel person would shut me out.

"The doors by the auditorium are open," she said. "Go there."

I wedged my foot in so the door wouldn't close. "It's all the way around the other side!" I said. "I'm not going to make it!"

The woman hesitated, then relented. "Go," she said, opening the door. "But come back to the office when you're done."

I made a show of running to the nearest washroom. After an appropriate interval, I emerged and sprinted to the office. The woman was only then hauling the cart away from the drop box.

Success! Every answer in the box would be logged as eight o'clock, and Hans-Peter's application would be safe. I left the office and headed out to the football stadium to check on the float.

That's when I heard the sirens.

Chapter 9

Digits

Freddie

The sirens grew steadily louder.

I wondered if something was happening at Navy Pier, until I saw a fire truck pull into the Peshtigo School parking lot. Which was where the floats were lined up. And smoke was rising.

Two more trucks roared into the lot before I reached it. Some of the floats were on fire. I couldn't tell which ones, because the fire trucks were blocking my view.

I reached a small crowd watching the flames do their work. Poseidon's Revenge and about three other floats were a charred mess. There was no fixing this. Hans-Peter's *T. rex* would never make it back to the basement.

The onlookers seemed to be Peshtigo staffers and three or four students who were putting last-minute touches on the floats. "What happened?" I asked.

"Ms. Murchison-Kowalski, please come with me," a voice at my shoulder said.

I turned around to see the unpleasant and unsmiling face of Vice-Principal Harrell.

"Wait, why?" I asked as we headed off to the office.

"Where were you at five minutes past eight?" Mr. Harrell wanted to know.

"Five after?" I asked, trying to think.

"That was when Ms. Shropshire called the fire department," Mr. Harrell said.

"I was —" I began, then suddenly realized he *really* thought I was responsible for the fire.

"I didn't do anything," I said.

"If I may ask, without being accusatory, then why are you here?" he replied. "Your float appeared to have been finished, and the parade isn't until noon."

"I'm here to drop off my cousin's Peshtigo School application test," I told him. "He couldn't do it because he hurt himself in a deli slicing accident." Then I realized just how that sounded.

"I assume you got it in on time?"

"I did *not* start the fire!" I protested.

Mr. Harrell frowned. "Even if you got the exam here as late as eight, you had enough time. You have a history of, shall we say, irregular conduct involving football stadiums."

I knew. Angus. Texas. Probation.

"But that we did for a reason," I told him. "To save a steer. This . . . why would we set our own float on fire?"

"I'm afraid I'm going to have to call your guardian," Mr. Harrell said.

∙❋∙

Hans-Peter

When I woke up, I was lying in a hospital bed. My left hand was bandaged. My mouth felt cottony and gross. A television was on, volume low, showing the local news.

Opa was sitting in an orange plastic chair by the bed, reading some magazine.

I groaned.

"How do you feel?" he asked, looking up. There was a tightness around his eyes.

I raised my hand. It was covered in bandages, and my ring finger was a *lot* shorter than it had been. It . . . it . . . Wow.

"They had to take off your finger at the first knuckle," Opa explained.

I twisted my hand back and forth and wiggled the fingers. "Call me Frodo," I said, then leaned back in bed.

"Who?" Opa asked.

"Never mind," I said. Then something occurred to me. "Wait," I asked, looking at my hand. "They took off part of my finger? Where is it? Do I get to keep it?"

"*Nein,* it went into the *sauerbraten,*" Opa said, definitely less tense now. His mouth twitched.

"Ugh," I said. Too gross. Too bad Freddie wasn't there to hear it. "Where's Freddie?" I was surprised she wasn't there. Full of commentary on the dangerous equipment used to rend animal flesh. But, more than that, I needed to find out if she got my test answer to the Peshtigo School in time.

"I do not know," he said. "I have been waiting for her to call."

I happened to glance at the television. On screen, a lady with a microphone was reporting live from the Peshtigo School.

I pointed. "Turn it up."

Opa grabbed the remote and raised the volume.

"*More about today's homecoming fire at the prestigious Peshtigo School when we return . . . ,*" Then she faded to a commercial about some prescription drug for either sinus headaches or lactose intolerance.

"You don't suppose . . . ," I began.

Opa was shaking his head. "Frederika, what have you done now?"

The bedside phone rang.

Opa answered it. "*Ja,*" he said. He was silent a long moment. "I see," he said. He was silent another long moment. "I will come pick her up," he said, then hung up.

"That was the Peshtigo School," he said, his voice

grim. "Frederika's float burned up before the parade. No one was hurt." He grabbed his jacket off the chair and opened the door. "If you are sure you are all right, I will be back."

With that, he left me with the local news. It seemed odd, the whole thing. I wondered what kind of statement Freddie was trying to make. When the TV news came back from commercial, the correspondent explained. *"Flames erupted from the mouth of a sea serpent and then engulfed the entire float . . ."*

"It was a *Tyrannosaurus rex*," I muttered, "not an icthyosaur."

I turned off the TV when the phone rang. It was my mom, calling from Japan. She'd gotten a message from Opa and she wanted to know if I was all right and what I had been thinking, using the slicing machine. I told her about everything that had been going on, and when I got off the phone, I began to wonder if getting in to the Peshtigo School was worth all this trouble. After all, I'd been nearly drowned in the fountain, attacked by bees, and now had a finger chopped off. Well, part of one. It wasn't really one of the important ones, but it was still a finger. And all the faculty I'd met so far were as freaky as Freddie.

Still, I'd come this far and there was that dinosaur dig in Montana. . . .

Freddie

I'd never seen Opa furious before.

Outraged, yes.

Upset, yes.

But never deeply, profoundly angry.

When he came to get me, he was polite to Mr. Harrell, but didn't make any chitchat or bad jokes. He was silent on the way to the car as well.

"What were you thinking?" he asked. "Were you thinking of anything?"

"I —" I began.

"I have been very tolerant," Opa interrupted.

"But —"

He held up a hand. "Very tolerant. You are intelligent and strong-willed, which are virtues . . . even when you insult me and my business with your animal-meat crusading. But this . . . this . . ." His voice trailed off.

"From now on," he said, "you will be spending your free time at the deli. *All* of your free time. None of this being excused for school functions." Opa glared at me. "You can help Mrs. Fraunhofer at the cash register, lifting and cleaning things."

Back home, exiled to my room, I threw myself onto my bed. It was depressing. After everything I'd done to bring attention to veganism, the event that had greatest effect — and not in a good way — wasn't anything I'd done. Or would have even considered doing.

I wasn't going to give up, though.

I would definitely continue to speak out about veganism.

It's just that it probably would be at a different school. Probation, Mr. Harrell had said. Kicked out of two schools in the same semester. Before mid-terms, even.

And I even liked the Peshtigo School.

But, no matter what, I was *not* going to ruin Hans-Peter's chances of getting in to the Peshtigo School by letting anyone know I hadn't gotten his test in on time. Hans-Peter. He was all right. Too much into the whole *wurst* thing, but I was making progress with him. At least he seemed to listen to me more than half the time.

And after all he'd been through, he still really seemed to want to go to the Peshtigo School. Sure, I'd miss it, but . . . me, I could be vegan anywhere. Eleanor could take over USCACA, if the administration didn't dissolve the organization.

I'd keep my mouth shut.

Chapter 10

Veganwurst

Hans-Peter

I was released from the hospital quickly — a finger amputation happens more often than you'd think, so it's usually an outpatient deal, apparently. The mood at home was surreal. Freddie was holed up in her room, and Opa was upstairs. Neither was speaking to the other. Even odder, Freddie wasn't speaking at all — she'd apparently never told Opa exactly what had happened with the homecoming float. And when I asked, she told me to mind my own business.

I was in my room, having failed to get interested in a new book on dinosaur hunting.

My finger or, I guess, my stump, didn't hurt too bad. It was still bandaged, of course, and I was still on painkillers, which I'd take every four-to-six hours, or when my whole hand started to throb.

But I had a lot of time to think. And what I thought about, unfortunately, was Freddie. Yeah, she was a pain and we'd had our differences, but the thing of it was, this whole spectacular float arson fiasco didn't seem like her style. Not after all the time she'd spent crafting her message. How would a fire help the fishes?

I looked over at my calendar. Wurstfest was only a few days away. With the bandage and oozing sore, any hand-mixing of ground meat would probably constitute a health code violation.

Unless Freddie assisted. And then, she might even unbend enough to talk.

I worked on a new recipe for the next hour or so before knocking on Freddie's door and entering.

She was lying on her bed writing a letter.

"How'd you like to help me put together an entry for the Wurstfest contest?" I asked.

When she ignored me, I got to the point. "It'll be vegan. I'm calling it 'sushi kielbasa.'"

Freddie

Hans-Peter spent most of the time we worked on the contest entry trying to less-than-subtly interrogate me on the homecoming fire. Still, his veganwurst idea had produced something quite edible: a weird mixture of vegetables wrapped in a sheet of seaweed. Very odd, but tasty. It gave me some hope that over the long term we could open the minds of even sausage-eaters to veganism.

Despite everything, Opa seemed to think the Wurstfest contest was a suitable activity for me, so I got to go, although that might also have had something to do with the fact that I had to help at the deli booth.

Wurstfest was set up like a big block party, with the street closed to traffic. One end served as a stage and dance area, for the bands and polka competitions. The other end had been kept more open, with the shops decorated brightly in black and red and yellow and blue, and with booths in the center of the street that either sold souvenirs or hooked people in to the real shops. In the center stood the Fest Hall, where the sausage judging would be. Not far off from that was the deli booth, where Hans-Peter and I would be handing out samples of Opa's traditional, Old World–style wurst and, I hoped, some of our fusion kielbasa. Opa and Mrs. Fraunhofer manned the deli itself.

It surprised me that Hans-Peter would be helping out, what with it having been only a few days since his amputation, but the doctor had said there was no gangrene.

After I installed Hans-Peter at the deli booth, I took our sushi kielbasa entry over to the Fest Hall. Inside, a half dozen folding tables had been covered with red-and-white-checked plastic tablecloth. Small metal holders held up signs indicating where to place your entry. Larger ones identified your category.

The judges gave awards for the categories like Amateur Sausage, Professional Sausage, and Youth. Sub-categories included Traditional, Exotic, Smoked, and the like. They also gave a Best-in-Show Award to the overall winner from the category winners. It looked like there would be about a hundred different entries.

Carrying mine, I glanced over at the Professional tables. Opa had already delivered his six entries and left. That made my job a lot easier. I didn't want to have to explain everything to him at the beginning of the day.

I found my place at the table in the Amateur Exotic category and set out the little silver metal tray with three sushi kielbasa rolls onto it. You were not allowed to slice it yourself, because the judges evaluated internal and external appearance, as well as taste.

Trying to decide how to arrange the stuff, I took a look around at the other entries. Near ours was something called a smoked shiitake mushroom and buffalo sausage. At the next table, some guy was putting out a spicy quail sausage that looked like it weighed about five pounds.

He saw me glance over and announced with a smile, "It's all white meat! I bagged 'em myself!"

Cringing, I took another look around. Our sushi kielbasa was definitely the only greenish black sausage in the entire room. Also the only one that was remotely vegetarian.

It was sad, really, and the smell was making me sick. I left as soon as I signed out at the judges' desk.

Hans-Peter and I stuck by the booth while he handed out samples of cold cuts and sausage, and we directed people to the store. By the end of the day, we were anxious for Mrs. Fraunhofer to relieve us so we could go listen to the contest announcements. When she finally arrived, we hustled over to the Fest Hall.

The place was packed. I was surprised at the number of people there.

The folding chairs had been rearranged to face a lectern with a microphone on top of a folding table. Seven judges sat behind another table next to the one with the lectern. Hans-Peter and I slipped onto a couple chairs at the back of the crowd. I didn't see Opa anywhere.

I wasn't sure how well the sushi kielbasa would go over with the judges, but thought, all else being objective, we'd done a good job. Certainly better than some of the gross entries I'd seen at check-in.

The awards for the Amateur Sausage Makers were first.

I didn't pay too much attention, although I did find it weird that there was a "Youth" category; the winner was nine years old, and how freakish was it that parents were starting the kiddies in on the slaughter that young?

Hans-Peter nudged my arm when the judges were set to announce the winner for "Amateur Exotic." I nudged him back because it wasn't like I wasn't paying attention.

"Third place in the category Amateur Exotic," the MC announced, "goes to Donald Burnham and his wild pheasant sausage."

As people applauded, Donald Burnham went up to collect his plaque.

"We have two more chances," I whispered to Hans-Peter.

"I know," he whispered back.

After Burnham had taken a few photos and gone back to his seat, the MC continued. "Our next award is for second place in Amateur Exotic. The winner is Mimi Kuhn, for her pork, apple, and pistachio sausage."

Other than the pork, that didn't sound terrible.

I grabbed Hans-Peter's arm. "One more."

"I know," he replied again, prying my fingers off his arm.

I scanned the crowd again.

"And the Grand Prize in the category Amateur Exotic goes to Rudy Euler and his Alsatian salami!"

"*What?*" I exclaimed, looking at the MC, then at the table of judges, and then at Hans-Peter. "What's so exotic about salami? Where is Alsatia, anyway?"

"Be quiet," Hans-Peter whispered, as we got funny looks from the guy sitting in front of us. "It's not Alsatia, it's Alsace-Lorraine."

I sighed.

Hans-Peter

The worst part about Wurstfest (pun intended) was the late-night cleanup at the deli, especially after spending most of the day at the booth.

Of course, Opa was in a good mood because he was ahead of last year's take and because he'd won the Professional contest.

Again.

Just before we left for the night, he grabbed a fax from the machine, quickly collated, then scanned the pages.

"This tells us nothing," he said after a minute.

"What is it?" I asked. Freddie was standing over by the door, trying to avoid Opa, which she'd been doing since the homecoming fire.

"The preliminary fire department report on the homecoming fire," Opa replied.

"How did you get that?" I asked.

"I called in a favor from Bernard," Opa said. "He knows someone."

"Can I see it?" I asked.

"*Ja*, here," Opa said, thrusting it into my hands as we headed to the car.

I followed slowly, reading it over.

"How did you like Wurstfest?" I asked Freddie, slipping the report into my coat pocket.

"Not enough to eat," she replied.

When we got home, I grabbed my dictionary. Finding the entry I wanted, I confronted Freddie in her room, sitting at her desk. Opa had already gone upstairs.

"Why are you pretending you started the fire?" I asked.

She stood in front of me and said, "I am not a liar!"

I handed her the fire report. "This came today," I said. She glanced at it indifferently, but paused, as I had, at "Cause of Fire."

"Who are you protecting?" I asked. "Shohei? Did he start it?"

"No!" Freddie said. "It wasn't Shohei."

"Then who?" I demanded.

She sat down again, blowing out a long breath. "You idiot, I'm protecting *you*."

"What? Why? I didn't have anything to do with the fire."

"Because," she explained. "I didn't get your exam in on time. I was four minutes late. Which was almost exactly the time they think the fire started, give or take a minute. But I had to have gotten it there before eight to have dropped off your exam on time, which gave me the chance to dash over and start the fire. They think."

"Oh," I said. "Wow." This was entirely unexpected. "Then who . . ."

"Who started it?"

I nodded.

"Probably Patrick Jarndyce," she said. "Or maybe it was just an accident."

I was quiet a second. "I . . . ," I said, slowly. "I appreciate what you're trying to do, but my getting into the Peshtigo School isn't worth —"

Freddie cut in. "If you so much as breathe a word to Opa or anyone at the Peshtigo School, so help me, I'll chop off the rest of your hand. Now get out of my room."

Hans-Peter

I was *not* going to let Freddie take the fall. Even if it meant I wouldn't get in to the Peshtigo School. It wasn't right. It just wasn't. She was family.

A little loopy and insane, but family.

I called Shohei. "How do I meet with Mrs. Ruth Talmadge?"

"The head of the admissions committee?" he asked. "You don't."

"You're my application liaison. Liaise," I said. "Nine o'clock tomorrow. Also, I want to see Mr. Jarndyce. Tell him I'll sign the release for the head injury." I hung up before Shohei could respond.

Later that evening, though, I got a call from Honoria, the girl from the Peshtigo School Student Court who'd come up to me after the fountain incident. She told me she'd gotten a call from Shohei and gave me some very helpful information on what to say at tomorrow's meeting.

Next morning, I went to Mrs. Talmadge's office to see her and Mr. Jarndyce. Mrs. Talmadge sat behind a tidy gray metal desk. Mr. Jarndyce sat next to me in one of the black leather White Sox chairs.

After initial greetings, I got right to the point. "I can prove Freddie didn't set the floats on fire."

Mrs. Talmadge glanced over at Mr. Jarndyce. "I think that's more an issue for the disciplinary committee than the admissions committee."

I nodded. "Except that my admission is why Freddie couldn't have been the one to set the fire."

"Why?" Mr. Jarndyce asked, leaning forward.

"Because Freddie was still delivering my answer to the test when the fire started. And even though it was registered as on-time, she didn't actually get it in until a few minutes after eight. Which means I probably won't be admitted, I know. But it also means she couldn't have set the fire."

"I see," Mrs. Talmadge said, tenting her fingers. "Anything else?"

She was taking the late test delivery too matter-of-factly, but I decided to continue for the moment.

"Are you missing any shellac?" I asked Mr. Jarndyce.

"How did you know —" he began, then stopped.

Mrs. Talmadge nodded. "Go ahead, James."

"Siobhan and Patrick were fighting this morning over some of her art supplies." He shrugged. "I guess Patrick had grabbed a couple cans of paint and shellac for use on the float."

I pulled out the fire department report Opa had had faxed over. "Was it a can of something called 'Smythe's Belgian Shellac'?"

"Yes," Mr. Jarndyce said. "It's very expensive."

"Because domestic shellac just isn't good enough?" Mrs. Talmadge asked, smiling slightly.

"How do you know what the name of the shellac was?" Mr. Jarndyce said.

"Because," I told them, "according to the fire department report on the Peshtigo School fire, they found a can of Smythe's Belgian Shellac in the shell of the dinosaur. It was used to start the fire."

"How did you get this so quickly?" Mrs. Talmadge asked.

I shrugged. "My grandfather knows people."

"Are you accusing Patrick of starting the fire?" Mr. Jarndyce demanded. "Because any one of those people could have grabbed the can. Including your cousin."

"Yes, any one of a lot of people could have grabbed the can," I said. "But not Freddie."

"Well, obviously," Mr. Jarndyce said, "you're trying to protect her —"

"No," I said, then paused. "Well, I am, but it still couldn't have been her."

"Why not?" Mrs. Talmadge asked, hushing Mr. Jarndyce.

"Because shellac is not vegan," I said.

"What?"

"It's made from the resinous secretion of something called the lac bug," I told them. "Freddie would never touch the stuff."

They both stared.

"You might have something there," Mrs. Talmadge said.

"Oh, for crying out loud —" Mr. Jarndyce began.

"No," Mrs. Talmadge interrupted. "James, you've never met the girl. She's extremely . . . principled."

When Mr. Jarndyce began to protest, Mrs. Talmadge held up her hand and continued, "So, please clarify how you think the fire started, then."

"I think it was an accident," I said. "Someone left some shellac uncovered on the float and someone else tossed in a match. The floats were sitting right at the edge of the parking lot, next to the bus stop. Really, it could have been anyone."

"Thank you," Mrs. Talmadge said. "We'll look into it."

As I got up to leave, she said, "One more thing, Mr. Yamada: I would suggest that you continue the application process."

I hesitated.

"The reason your test answer was logged in as having been received on time was that it was. With about one minute to spare, in fact."

"But it was four, five minutes late," I said.

She shook her head. "No, it wasn't."

"I don't understand."

"Mr. Bellini was trying a little too hard to be clever," Mrs. Talmadge said. She looked pained. "You obviously assumed that he meant the exam was due twenty-four hours from the originally scheduled start time for the exam, eight o'clock. However, he didn't actually start the clock until ten minutes past eight, which was when he gave you the problem. He also told you that it was due exactly one *sidereal* day later. For our purposes, a sidereal day is twenty-three hours and fifty-six minutes long. Which means it was due at eight-oh-six the next morning." She smiled. "So make sure you finish your essays."

Then the smile was gone. "Of course, if the exam had started at eight AM, you would've had only until seven-fifty-six, not eight, to get it there and Freddie would've been eight minutes late." She leaned forward. "Try not to cut it so close next time."

I left. I wasn't sure whether I was happy or not. I think I'd convinced them about Freddie, but I'd already psyched myself into thinking I wouldn't have to finish the essays.

The Peshtigo School was a confusing place.

Freddie

I was dusting the Polish crystal when Hans-Peter got back to the deli.

"Guess what," he demanded.

"You told them everything, and now your chances of getting in to the Peshtigo School are deader than those dinosaurs you wanted to study," I said.

"Has anyone ever told you you are no fun at all?" he asked.

"Often," I replied.

This silenced him, but only for a moment.

"Actually, they believed me and are looking into other potential perpetrators," he said smugly. "And, since you did in fact get the test in on time, I'm still eligible for admissions. So there."

"What?"

He started to explain something about sidereal days that he didn't seem all that clear on. I really didn't get it either, so I simply asked, "Do you want to tell Opa, or should I?"

Hans-Peter flashed me a grin, then went to see Opa in his office.

He came back a couple minutes later, Opa in tow.

"So," Opa said, nodding, "I was right. You are not so stupid as to burn down your school. Again."

"Hey!" I said, starting to protest, as Hans-Peter began laughing — possibly for the first time — at one of Opa's jokes.

I was still slightly annoyed, but figured this was as close to an apology as I was going to get.

"Come," Opa said. "We will go to Konditerei Schmedes." He grabbed his jacket off the coathook, and made pushing gestures.

"Opa . . . ," I said.

"You can have a coffee and the *birnenkompott*," he explained. "They are vegan. I checked."

"The stewed pears?" I asked. "But those are only good over ice cream."

"*Ja*, I know," he said. "But Erika was telling me they have some new frozen flavored soybean emulsion or something."

I was relieved. Me and Opa, we were good now.

"Um, guys," Hans-Peter said. He held up his bandaged hand. "I'm going to take a pass. You two go ahead. I think I need to work on my application essays . . ."

Opa gave him a look before we headed out. "By the way. That sushi kielbasa of yours? It was not terrible."

Hans-Peter

PESHTIGO SCHOOL APPLICATION ESSAY NO. 3
Describe something you've built.

Sushi Kielbasa

A good sausage requires the artful combination of three elements: fresh ingredients, piquant seasoning mixture, and a suitably chosen skin material. (While skinless "sausage patties" are known, these are more akin to a hamburger patty than a proper sausage.)

Sausage skin generally comes in edible and non-edible forms. Of the edible kinds, the most popular are (a) the (thoroughly cleaned) intestines of sheep or hogs, and (b) collagen (an animal protein that forms the basic structure of skin, connective tissue, etc., in vertebrates). As can be appreciated, neither is vegan.

Non-edible choices include muslin (a coarse cotton fabric); cellulose (a plant fiber); or a variety of synthetics.

Thus, the requirement of a suitable edible skin material has been problematic in allowing vegans to partake of the culinary marvel that is the sausage.

Until now.

The Recipe:
   1 lb Portobella or wild mushrooms
   2/3 cup chopped yellow onion
   2 cloves garlic, minced
   1/2 cup cilantro, chopped
   2 avocados, chopped
   1 1/2 T extra virgin olive oil
   1 can black beans (drained and rinsed) or
      equivalent, cooked
   1 t salt

1 t thyme

1 t sage

1/2 cup (vegan) bread crumbs

1 T lemon juice

nori (dried seaweed) sheets

2+ cups brown rice

1. Steam rice, then set aside.
2. Preheat oven to 450°F.
3. Coat mushrooms, onion, and garlic in oil and roast for 10 minutes.
4. Chop mushrooms, onion, garlic, black beans, avocadoes, salt and seasonings, and cilantro in food processor.
5. After chopping, mix with bread crumbs.
6. Mix two parts mixture with one part steamed brown rice; roll in nori sheet.
7. Roast in 450° oven for 10–15 minutes.

Note: The mixture (before combining with rice) also makes an excellent vegetable dip.

Chapter 11

News

Hans-Peter

When you think about it, it's a little odd that it costs the same to send a piece of mail from Hawaii to Chicago as it does to send the same piece of mail from Chicago 60611 to Chicago 60625. It's also odd that it takes roughly the same amount of time for it to be delivered.

Not that I was waiting at the mail slot or anything. I mean, I knew when the acceptance letters were going out, and I knew, roughly, how long it would take for such a document to go from the Peshtigo School to the main post office down on Congress Avenue, from there be taken to be distributed locally, and then be walked slowly over to my street by Carl, our letter carrier, who had gotten his job from the first Mayor Daley.

Besides, the first I'd see the mail would be when I got home from the deli. Which was why it was totally unjustified of Freddie to tell me, late October, that I was driving her crazy, checking the mail all the time.

Still, to keep my mind off it, I was trying to learn to type again, with only nine fingers. S and W were kind of hard, because I kept trying to stab them when no fingertip was there to connect with the keys.

Finally, though, the envelope with the Peshtigo letterhead arrived. It was small and thin and expensive-looking. Freddie had warned me it might be thin, though, because if I was accepted, the administrative information wouldn't come until later.

I'd just gotten home from the deli with Opa and Freddie, unlocked the back door, and walked, not run, to the front hall, where Baschi was lying on the mail and chewing on a kitchen equipment catalog.

I tore open the envelope and unfolded the letter.

"Yes!" I shouted. "I got in!"

Opa whooped out a *"Wunderbar!"*

"Congratulations," Freddie said, with a small grin. "I never doubted."

I was rereading the letter as the phone rang.

Freddie picked it up. "Hello? Shohei! What . . . no, I don't have plans this weekend." I guessed she would want privacy and so left her there with the phone.

"Let me see," Opa said, as I sat back and relaxed.

Finally.

As he was reading, Freddie came into the kitchen. "Hans-Peter, your mom's on call-waiting."

She paused, smiling.

I was instantly suspicious. "And?" I asked as she held out the phone.

She covered the mouthpiece. "She and your father got back together!" she blurted. "And guess what?"

"What?"

She actually hugged me. And *squealed.* "You're going to be having a sister!"

Epilogue

From the *Peshtigo Weekly Penguin:*

PESHTIGO SCHOOL, CHICAGO — The Peshtigo School Student Court found Patrick Jarndyce guilty last Friday of malicious hooliganism in connection with the now-infamous fire that destroyed multiple homecoming parade floats. The defendant is greatly vexed in consequence.

Jarndyce confessed to starting the fire on the Union of Students Concerned About Cruelty to Animals (USCACA) float but claims it was an accident. "He was trying to create the illusion of a fire-breathing dragon," says Public Defender Honoria Grob, "and the pyrotechnics just got out of control." She added that the incident had no relationship to an alleged intra-organizational rivalry between Jarndyce and fellow USCACA member Frederika Murchison-Kowalski, as had been argued by prosecutor Christopher "Goliath" Reed. Although Murchison-Kowalski was briefly a suspect in the case, she was cleared of any involvement before trial and had no comment.

Jarndyce plans to appeal.

Author's Note

The flavor of *Tofu and T. rex* was inspired by my childhood, growing up in a German-American neighborhood on Chicago's North Side. Like Hans-Peter, my family is Japanese-German-American (although his family is also part Polish). My father immigrated to the United States from Germany in his late teens.

The story is set in a fictitious German-American neighborhood called "Little Swabia." The setting is largely based on the Lincoln Square neighborhood, though greatly expanded. It also owes some texture to German-American towns such as Fredericksburg, Texas; New Braunfels, Texas; and Frankenmuth, Michigan. Like many German-American neighborhoods and towns, the distinctions between regions of Germany are somewhat blurred and, being set in Chicago, there is also a strong Polish influence.

Opa, Freddie, and Hans-Peter live in one of the more than eighty thousand "Chicago-style bungalows" built during the housing boom of the early twentieth century. According to the Chicago Bungalow Initiative, these homes comprise more than one third of all Chicago single-family homes. More information on these houses can be found at www.chicagobungalow.org.

In *Tofu and T. rex,* Shohei takes Hans-Peter to meet with Dr. Lee at the Field Museum of Natural History (www.fieldmuseum.org). The museum was originally established to house artifacts from the World's Columbian Exposition of 1893. It has been at its present location near the Shedd Aquarium and Adler Planetarium since 1921 and is one of the world's premier institutions of its kind. Its paleontology collection includes Sue, one of the most complete *Tyrannosaurus rex* skeletons ever found. To the best of my knowledge, however, they have never had an exhibit of Rose Parade floats.

Sausage, as Hans-Peter mentions, has an ancient pedigree. Homer mentions sausage in *The Odyssey,* for example, although it likely goes back at least as far the domestication of the pig.

Veganism is of a somewhat more recent vintage. The vegan movement apparently began formally in 1944 in England, with the founding of the Vegan Society and promulgation of a Vegan Manifesto.

The history of pi would take many volumes to fill. Many poem mnemonics have been developed in a variety of languages. The use of a ten letter word to represent a zero digit in pi appears fairly standard (although some use it as an excuse to end the exercise entirely.).

In his effort to be clever, Mr. Bellini bases his exam deadline on "one sidereal day . . . no eccentricities," which Mrs. Talmadge calls twenty-four hours and fifty-six minutes. Why?

A sidereal day is the amount of time it takes the earth to make one complete rotation on its axis. A solar day is the amount of time between meridian passages of the sun (that is, the time between the sun being directly overhead one day to the next). The solar day is longer than the sidereal day because the earth is traveling around the sun at the same time it is rotating on its axis. Because of this, the earth has to make slightly more than one revolution (which takes about four minutes) for the sun to be overhead at noon the next day. (In actuality, other factors, including the tilt of the earth's axis and the fact that the earth's orbit is not completely circular, also affect the duration of the day. Mr. Bellini deals with these by ignoring them and specifying that the determination is to be made assuming no eccentricities.)

Finally, and sadly, the Peshtigo School does not exist. If it did, it would be located in Chicago's Streeterville neighborhood, at the corner of Peshtigo and Grand, the site of the old Kraft Building.

Pronunciation Note

Hans-Peter — hahntz PAY-ter

Honoria — *ah-NOR-ee-ah*

Shohei — show-hay

Willi — VILL-ee (short for *Wilhelm*)

Acknowledgments

The author would like to thank the following:

For reading early drafts and excerpts of the manuscript,
Anne Bustard, Sean Petrie, and my wife, Cynthia;

For allowing me to wander around with a camera, the
proprietors of Delicatessen Meyer, Chicago, Illinois;

For being skilled docents of the Peshtigo School,
my editor, Amy Hsu, and my agent, Ginger Knowlton.

About the Author

Greg Leitich Smith grew up in a German American neighborhood on Chicago's North Side. He drew on his own heritage and experiences at a science magnet high school (much like the Peshtigo School) in writing *Tofu and T. rex*. He holds degrees in electrical engineering from the University of Illinois at Urbana-Champaign and the University of Texas at Austin, and a University of Michigan degree in law. He now lives with his wife, children's author Cynthia Leitich Smith, and their four cats in Austin, Texas. Greg's Web site is *www. gregleitichsmith.com.*

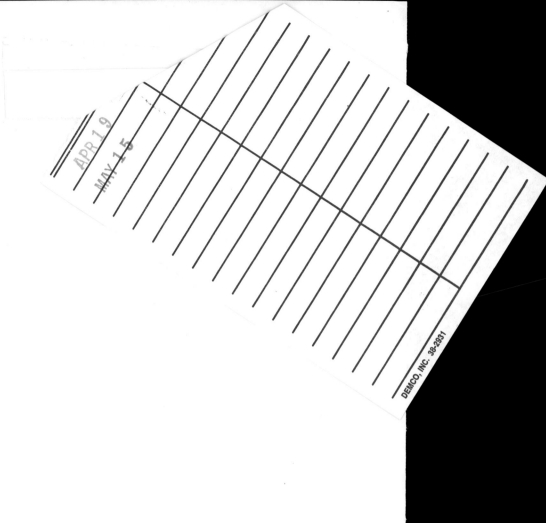